CW00410355

Because of Lila

#1 *NEW YORK TIMES* BESTSELLING AUTHOR

ABBI GLINES

Because of Lila
Published by Abbi Glines
Copyright © 2017 by Abbi Glines

Abbi@Abbiglines.com

Interior Design & Formatting by:
Christine Borgford, Type A Formatting
www.typeAformatting.com

All rights reserved. Published in the United States by Abbi Glines. This is a work of fiction. Names, characters, places and incidents either are the product of the author's imagination or are used fictitiously. Any resemblance to actual persons, living or dead, events, or locales, is entirely coincidental.

Because of Lila

Prologue

THE SAME. EVERY get together was always the same. The people and the scenery never change. Repeat, repeat, repeat.

I sighed and tried to keep a pleasant expression on my face. It was easy enough. I'd mastered it over the years. Smile, answer their questions, act interested in their life, and move on. Those were the survival steps required to get through an event among the Rosemary Beach elite.

As a child, it was fun. I played with the other kids. We found things to entertain us and our parents didn't mind too much when Nate Finlay or Cruz Kerrington led us astray. It was easily exciting. Not a dull moment. But then puberty came and it all changed.

I turned my head to look at my parents. My father was handsome and didn't look like a man on the back side of his forties. He was loved by this crowd, as was my mother, who I had always believed was beautiful. My father kept his hand on the small of her back, and the love in their eyes as they spoke to each other was real. You could see it. No one could question it—their love oozed from them.

Being raised by two people who had lived a fairytale romance set my relationship expectations a little high. No, make that ridiculously high. I wanted what they had and believed it was a given that I'd have a great romance too. The heartbreak of that notion is that at the age of twenty-two I had still never been in love. I'd thought I loved Cruz Kerrington once. We were kids. He'd kissed me, and I saw that fairytale in my future. Then the next week he'd kissed Melanie Harnett, and my fourteen-year-old heart was crushed.

That wasn't the end of my dream, though. Cruz would flirt and wink. Come up beside me in the halls at school and whisper things in my ear. But he never did it in front of anyone. Girl after girl was on his arm, in his arms, and in the backseat of his BMW. Slowly, Cruz managed to disillusion me and the dream in my head.

"You've been quieter than normal tonight," Caspian Manning, my cousin, said to me as he took the seat beside me. He was rarely at these events since he lived in Fort Worth. But mom had said he wanted to transfer to a college in Florida. She was hopeful he'd move here. I never imagined him anywhere else except Uncle Mase's ranch, but he wanted something else from life. I could tell him Florida was a bad choice. *Go west.*

"A lot on my mind," I said with less of my fake smile since he knew me too well.

He smirked. "Like how much longer until you can go home and hole up with a book in your room?"

I gave a small lift on my left shoulder then gave him my own smirk. "Mostly."

He leaned back and crossed his arms over his chest. "Reckon these people ever think about leaving this place? These balls or whatever shit this is y'all do, all seem the same. Nothing exciting but that shrimp dip over there."

"It's a fundraiser for Dyslexia. Your parents are two of the sponsors. Don't be a snot." His mother, my Aunt Reese, had dyslexia for years and didn't know it. Once she realized what her problem was she learned to read and finished school. She was a real inspiration.

"Yeah, I know. I get it, but last month there was another party here and the month before that. We always get the invitations. I see them on the kitchen counter. Fancy ass paper and gold wax stamp sealing the back," Caspian said with a sigh and then surveyed the room from where we stood.

I wanted to agree with him but I kept my mouth shut. Last month was the annual cotillion where the girls who have come of age are presented to society. It's so incredibly outdated, yet they still do it every year. I did cotillion when I was their age—I still have nightmares.

"Someone needs to take the booze away from Cruz. The dude looks like he's bordering on tipsy headed to smashed."

That, unfortunately, caught my attention. I followed his gaze and saw Cruz laughing a little too loudly and swaying a bit. I quickly checked the room for either of his parents and didn't notice them. They would be very upset, and it would cause a scene. This would have been a good time for Nate to step in. But Nate wasn't here. He was in Alabama with his fiancée where he now lived.

I waited a minute to see if anyone around him was going to do something when another drink was placed in his hands by a server. Not good.

"I better do something. His parents will be humiliated if he ruins this event."

"Good luck," was Caspian's response as I reluctantly headed toward Cruz.

I didn't go near Cruz for good reasons. However, his parents owned this place. Kerrington Country Club was theirs. If Cruz got crazy and did something ridiculous, I'd feel terrible for them. As much as I didn't care for him, I liked his parents very much.

Before I reached him, he had handed his nineteen-year-old brother Blaze his drink and taken another from the tray. Two Kerrington boys getting drunk was even worse. I may never forgive Nate for moving, because for the first time in years I was forced to interact with Cruz.

Avoiding him had become a talent. A talent I was rather proud to possess.

I walked up unnoticed and snatched the glass right out of Blaze's hand before he could tilt it back for a sip. "Don't think so," I said placing the full glass on a waiter's tray before turning to Cruz who was watching me with an amused but confused grin. "As for you, let's get out of here before you do something stupid. No wait, you've already given bourbon to a nineteen-year-old— before you can do anything else stupid."

Cruz laughed then. "I don't think we've met. I'm Cruz Kerrington, and you are?" He was mocking me.

"Don't be an ass," I replied with a scowl.

He threw his head back and laughed loudly. Too loudly. When he met my gaze again his eyes were still laughing at me. "I can't believe that Lila Kate Carter just said the word 'ass.'"

Why had I liked him once? Did I actually think I had loved him at the time? God, I was dumb when I was younger. "Cruz. Please. Let's go." I grabbed his arm to force him out when Chanel—whose last name I couldn't remember, but that first name was hard to forget—stepped in front of me.

"Where are you going, Cruz?" Chanel asked. "We had plans."

He shrugged. "Don't know. Ask Lila Kate." He didn't pull away from me. He seemed to be enjoying the awkward situation instead.

Chanel's large brown eyes snapped away from Cruz to look

at me. She was angry. I didn't care. If she wanted to get Cruz out of here she was welcome to. "We've already made plans. He's taken," she all but growled at me.

"If your plans include getting him out of here, then please take him. He's had too much to drink, and he needs to leave."

"He can do whatever he wants. He's a Kerrington."

"Can I just say that I'm enjoying this immensely." Cruz's speech was now a little slurred.

"Just take him and leave." I was tired of this. I wanted to walk back and sit quietly at my table. Dance with whoever asked, and be polite until I was safely in my room again.

"Don't tell me what to do! I don't care who your grandfather is. He's retired. You're so high and mighty. Stop acting like that makes you more important."

Was she really going there? Jeez. I hadn't dealt with that accusation in years. My grandfather was the lead singer of the legendary rock band Slacker Demon. They had stopped touring years ago—I don't even remember when that happened it had been so long.

"I've changed my mind. I want Lila Kate to take me. I'm bored with you," Cruz said. "And you're mean."

What? I jerked my gaze from Chanel to Cruz who was still grinning like a drunken idiot. "You're more fun. Let's go."

"Are you serious?" Chanel screeched an octave higher. "She's a boring goody-goody."

"She's real, Chanel. She's fucking real," he said calmly, and then he smirked at me. "You better get me outta here before I cause that scene."

I didn't argue. I was annoyed, but I didn't argue. I didn't take his arm this time. I just led the way out of the ballroom and outside the building. Away from the valet, because there was no way he was getting in his car and driving. I took him to the clubhouse instead. I figured he could sleep it off in there on one of the many large expensive leather sofas.

"Where are we headed? Are you taking me to the tenth hole to have your way with me?"

I knew he was joking. But it still got under my skin. "Not interested in having any way with you. Just saving Woods and Della the headache of their oldest acting like a moron in front of everyone."

He chuckled. "God, you're always so good. That's sexy you know that? Your angelic face, killer body and perfect manners. It's a combination that guys fantasize about—to get you to be wild. Taste some freedom."

"I have plenty freedom," I managed to say, although his description of me was a little startling.

"The untouchable Lila Kate Carter," he continued. "So desirable and so freaking icy cold that you can't get close."

Icy cold? I wasn't icy cold.

"Excuse me?"

I stopped at the steps leading up to the clubhouse and glared at him with disbelief.

"You," he said running a finger under my chin, "are an expensive china doll that can only be seen and not touched. It's so tempting, but you know that if you try, it will shatter. So you don't break it. You stay back. Admire from a distance. Until you've had too much to drink and you give in a little. Just to be near her."

I didn't like this. Not any of it. I wasn't a breakable doll. I was very strong. I wasn't emotional or dramatic. I was tough. I was obedient. I was a rule follower. That didn't make me cold. "Just because I don't get drunk, party and sleep with every guy in town doesn't make me cold," I shot back at him.

"No, but you've never gotten close to any guy. That verges on icy."

"I am not!" I raised my voice. That wasn't fair.

"Really? Then how about this?" he said just before he wrapped his arm around my back and pulled me to him. The whiskey on his tongue was the first thing I tasted as he kissed me. He did it like he was trying to force me to react. Like he was pushing me for more. He did it like he didn't mean it at all. His hand squeezed my waist painfully and nothing about this moment was sweet or romantic.

I placed both my hands on his chest and pushed him back. He staggered back easily then shook his head with a smile. "See. I told you."

"Cruz!" Chanel's voice screamed.

Both our heads turned to see her storming toward us in heels so high that it was impressive she was so agile in them and didn't break her neck. I would fall over.

"Well, Chanel, you found me. Good," he pointed his thumb at me. "This one isn't gonna work out. So, you get to go into this clubhouse with me and show me those red panties you said you weren't wearing."

Chanel looked smug. Like she'd won a prize that we had been competing for.

"You left me in there," she pouted.

"Had to try out the other option. It was delicious but needs a little thawing for my taste," Cruz drawled as he looked at me with hooded eyes. "Goodnight, Lila Kate."

They walked into the clubhouse with his hand on her bottom. She was already kissing his neck. It was that easy for him. And he was that shallow.

His awful behavior was not what I wanted. If fairytales weren't real, then I wanted adventure. Which meant I had to leave Rosemary Beach.

It was time.

Chapter One

♥ LILA KATE ♥

THE MONEY THAT my grandfather had deposited in my trust fund remained untouched. I had gone to a private college on a scholarship for dance a little over an hour from here. I had been in private dance classes since I was three years old and had asked my dad if I could wear a tutu and twirl around on a big stage one day.

Originally, my dream had been to open a dance academy here in Rosemary Beach. But over the years that had changed. The more the fairytale in my head began to crumble, so did that idea. I didn't want to travel the world and spend endless hours chasing a dream to be a famous dancer. I saw the dedication that went into it. I had friends who had gone on to do just that. It was all they had time for. It was their life. I wanted something else.

This past May, I had graduated with a Major in Literature and a Minor in Dance. I was still trying to figure out exactly what I was going to do with my degree, and what path I wanted to pursue. Nothing seemed right. Instead, I spent my time looking at condos to buy with some of my trust fund money. Living with my parents at twenty-two years old, almost twenty-three wasn't exactly a goal of mine.

My idea to leave and find adventure had been exciting. But standing on the front porch of the house that had always been my home with a suitcase by my side and my parents hugging me goodbye was harder than I had imagined it would be.

"Call me. When you get to Sea Breeze, call me from Nate's. Please," my mom said as she held me tightly. As cliché as it may sound my mother was my best friend. I never went through a rebellious stage where I hated my parents or thought they knew nothing. I'd gone to my mother about all my problems.

"I will. And I'll let you know my next stop as soon as I figure it out," I assured her. I had a friend in Birmingham, Alabama who had taken a teaching position at the Alabama School of Fine Arts. She wanted me to come for a visit. But I wasn't sure if I was going to keep driving along the Gulf Coast or take that northward turn on my journey.

"Tires are new, oil is changed, and it's been completely looked over," my dad said as he nodded at my silver Land Rover that had been a college graduation gift from my mother's father. "If any light comes on, take it directly to the nearest Rover dealer," his voice was tight with emotion he was trying hard to conceal. My mother was my best friend, but my father was my hero. I'd told him so at two years old, and it was still true today.

I moved to hug him tightly. "Thank you. I love you, Daddy," I said feeling tears sting my eyes. He held onto me as if he could keep me here forever.

"I love you, baby girl." His deep voice cracked when he spoke. I blinked hard to fight back the tears threatening to spill. They didn't need to see me cry. I wanted to do this. I needed to.

"I knew this day would come. We raised you to believe in yourself. Find what makes you happy and go get it. I couldn't be prouder of the woman you've become."

His words did not help me as I struggled not to cry. I swallowed hard and nodded my head against his chest. Then inhaled deeply, pulled myself together, and released him. I couldn't stay here in this safe world where my dad took care of me and find my life.

"I am who I am because of you two," I told them with a smile. "I'll be fine. And I'll call with updates regularly."

Mom sniffled then and gave me a soft smile. "Go find your happiness. You may look like me, but you are so much braver than I was. I wish I'd been as brave at your age."

My mother was the bravest woman I knew. She'd faced death to bring me into this world. She didn't consider that brave though. No matter how many times I told her it was. Especially when we sat and read my letters together. The ones she'd written me when she was pregnant. In case she didn't survive. Over the years we'd opened them and read them at the designated time. Dad had read them with us at first, but I had been little when I saw him leave the room quickly when mom began reading aloud. He didn't read them with us again.

She'd patted my head and smiled. "It's okay. He is happy that we're all together and these just remind him that we are blessed that's all."

I didn't understand when we had read the letters, but I did after a few years. The letters had reminded my dad of the hardest time in his life—when he thought he'd have to live this life without my mom. I couldn't imagine living life without her. I understood his pain. I never mentioned them in front of him again.

Dad picked up my suitcase. "Can't believe this is all you've packed."

"I travel light," I told him.

"And here I thought I was going to turn your bedroom into

my private gym. You've left everything behind." Now he was teasing me.

I shrugged and tried to appear playful. "I wanted to make sure it was all still here, and you that wouldn't forget me when I decided to come home finally."

Dad put my suitcase in the back of my Rover.

"We'd never touch your room. You know that," Mom said seriously.

I laughed. "I know." Although I never planned on moving back. For now, this was all I needed.

"Be careful, Lila Kate. We love you very much," she said as I hugged her one more time then headed to the driver's side where my dad already had the door open waiting for me.

"Don't stop at service stations that aren't busy and well lit. Try to get there before it's dark. You got your pistol under the seat?"

"Yes, Daddy. It's there. I'll be careful," I assured him.

With another hug, I climbed inside the Rover and drove away. I looked in my rearview mirror to see my parents waving from the front yard. My swing still hung from the tree there like it had my entire life. My world where I'd always known comfort—in this town where I only found the same emptiness every day—faded away behind me as I drove west.

I turned on the Bluetooth in my car and then found the travel playlist on my phone I'd put together last night. I felt free. Excited. I didn't feel like me. I didn't want to feel like me anymore. I didn't want to be labeled as prim and proper. Or icy . . . icy was the worst.

I'd thought about Cruz's drunken words and realized they had been true. And I hated him for saying them as much as I hated him for being right. I didn't want to be that girl. I wanted to be different. Take chances. Find my adventure.

Reaching for my bottle of water I sang along to the music.

The girl everyone met from now on would be a much different

Lila Kate Carter.

I would never be labeled proper or cold again. I'd be fun, exciting, ready for anything. The idea made me somewhat nervous, but it also gave me a thrill I hadn't experienced before.

Bring on my new life. Every crazy, wild, disorganized bit of it.

Chapter Two

♥ LILA KATE ♥

SEA BREEZE, ALABAMA was similar to Rosemary, but it was completely different. The beaches looked the same. Sea Breeze and Rosemary were on the same coast. However, the town of Sea Breeze was . . . well . . . less structured. There was no country club, and the stores weren't high end. There were souvenir stores with large tacky floats outside and airbrushed t-shirts that you would never see along the streets of Rosemary Beach. I loved it. The realness. The neon yellow signs flashing Free Hermit Crabs and Twenty-Four-Hour Breakfast and All You Can Eat Shrimp made me feel like I was in another world already.

My GPS was programmed to lead me to Nate's, but they weren't expecting me until later. I wanted to explore first. And to have some time to myself before I had to talk about my plans yet again. And Nate would ask. My actions were so out of character for me that I was expecting him to ask a lot of questions.

I made a quick call to let Mom know I made it to Sea Breeze safely, was doing some shopping and exploring, and that I'd call when I got to Nate's later. That way she'd relax and stop worrying.

I decided to drive around until I saw another neon sign that said Live Music and Fresh Crab, so I turned in. It was almost six o'clock, and I had told Nate and Bliss I would eat dinner before I got there. This looked like a good place to stop. The building was crowded already, so I could just blend in.

The music could be heard pouring from the speakers inside out into the parking lot. It wasn't bad. Not my thing but then I was changing me so I should learn to enjoy this kind of thing. Walking inside, I realized this was a bar. I was second guessing my decision to eat here when I realized that was an old Lila Kate way of thinking. The new Lila Kate was good with bar food. She'd try it.

The tables surrounding the place were tall with stools. They were also packed with girls in tiny shorts, halter tops and some wearing their bikini tops. Summer was over, but it was still hot outside. Fall didn't arrive until late October here. Tourists still came to the area, but the way everyone seemed to know each other, I wondered if this was the local crowd.

I decided to take one of the empty spots at the bar. The bartender was female which made me feel more relaxed. I sat down and turned back once to glance around. I watched the band on stage and took in the way the people acted. It was like some of the bars I'd gone to with friends when I was in college. I had never fit in there. But I would here. I was determined.

"What can I get for you?" I swung my attention back around to see the stunning bartender smiling at me. Her hair was a shade of red people paid good money for, and her eyes were an icy green that made me envious.

"Uh, yes. A menu perhaps?" I replied.

That response got a large grin from her. "Yeah, okay." She slid one over to me. "You look that over, and I'll be back. Unless, you know, you want to order a drink right now?"

"Oh, no, I need a moment. Thank you."

She started to walk off then paused. "You're not from here, are you?"

I shook my head. "No."

She seemed amused. "Didn't think so. If you've got any questions holler. My name's Larissa."

"Yes, okay. Thank you, Larissa."

I studied the menu. Crab nachos—I'd never heard of that combination. Did they make nachos with crab on them? It sounded like an excellent idea. Fried pickles, I'd seen those at bars before, but I'd never tasted them. Dancers had to keep their weight in check. Fried foods were off limits. I thought about trying that. Redneck caviar, now that sounded intriguing. But I wasn't a fan of black-eyed peas, and it didn't seem anything like caviar to me.

"Try the loaded potato skins with crab meat. Greasy as hell, and not at all healthy, but so damn good," a male voice said close by, startling me. I jumped a little and dropped the menu.

I turned my attention to him, and my breath caught a little. He was blonde, tall, tanned, well built and his smile was something. He also smelled good. Like soap and . . . whiskey. But it was a good combination.

He picked up my menu and handed it back to me. "I've been eating at this bar since before it was legal for me to get inside. Trust me. Go with the potato skins."

I nodded. I should say something witty or flirty, but I had nothing. I was sucking at this new Lila Kate thing. "Okay," was my wonderful response. Just "okay." What was wrong with me? I had seen attractive men all my life. Why was this one making it hard for me to talk?

"Larissa!" he called out, and the redhead turned to look at him with a frown that reached her forehead.

"What, Eli?" She didn't move from her position at the bar.

He looked at me. "What's your name?"

That I could answer easily enough. "Lila," I replied deciding that the new Lila Kate was going to drop that Kate. That name was silly and it made me sound ten years old. Lila was . . . sexier.

He gave me a crooked grin. "Lila. I like that. Fits you." Then he turned back to Larissa. "Lila here wants the potato skins loaded with crab."

Larissa walked over to us. "I see you're making friends," she said to Eli and then smiled at me. "He's had a little too much tonight. I'd cut him off but trust me this is a rarity for him. Anyway, did he order for you because he's planning on eating your food, or do you want the loaded potatoes?"

Everyone knew each other here. How nice. It was like a television show. "Yes, he has sold me on them. They sound delicious."

Larissa chuckled. "Don't set your hopes too high. They're good but delicious may be pushing it. What about a drink?"

Normally, I'd order bottled water. Instead, I said, "Dirty martini please."

"Got ID?"

I reached for my purse and took out my license then handed it to her. She glanced at it and nodded then looked at the guy beside me. "Behave," she said before walking off behind the bar.

He sat down on the stool beside me and leaned back against the bar looking out over the crowd. "I've never seen you here before. Where are you from Lila?"

I started to say Rosemary Beach but stopped myself. I didn't know this guy. He was a stranger. I wanted to live free and wild, but I needed to be careful to a certain degree.

"Florida," I replied instead. It was a big state. I could be vague.

He nodded. "Florida, huh? I was assuming you were on vacation, but if you're from Florida, I doubt that. Why vacation at this beach when you have beautiful ones there? What brings you to Alabama?"

I liked his voice. It was soothing. It paired nicely with the way he smelled—very appealing. "I'm traveling west. Going on an adventure of sorts."

He turned to look at me then. "An adventure? Alone?"

Okay, that was a bad idea. I shouldn't tell a strange guy I was alone. "No, I'm traveling with friends," I lied quickly.

He didn't look convinced. "Really?"

I nodded. "Yes, really."

"Dirty martini," Larissa said placing the drink I ordered in front of me. It had the ice slivers in it that I loved.

"Thank you. This looks wonderful."

"She's the best," Eli agreed. "Now how about another Jack?" he asked her.

"How about a glass of water first," she said sliding a glass of water in front of him.

"You're killing my buzz, Larissa," he said looking unhappily at his glass of water.

"I'm saving your ass," she told him. Then she turned and said to me over the music that was growing louder, "Eli's a nice guy. Better when he's sober. And your food will be out in five," she said holding up her hand with her five fingers spread.

I figured he had the approval of the bartender who seemed nice enough. I wasn't going to be abducted or raped tonight. That was a relief.

Chapter Three

~ELI HARDY~

TOO MUCH ALCOHOL was never a good thing. Unless you were home alone with pizza, or even better, Chinese food and the box set of Rocky DVDs. Then you were safe. But I'd been sworn off women for three weeks. The last women I had dated had made a wedding planner by the sixth date and proceeded to show it to me. That had been our last date.

I missed women. I'll admit it. The one sitting next to me was gorgeous, and she reminded me of that etiquette book my grandmother made Larissa read when we were kids. Grandma tried to make me read that book, but I wasn't doing it. I pretended. The picture of the girl on the front of the book was so polished and polite—that look hadn't been attractive until now. Wrapped up in this package beside me, it was a complete turn on.

Watching her attempt to eat a potato skin with a fork and knife was priceless. Larissa's face when she asked for "flatware" had been even better. We had grown up around my grandmother, so we were used to proper people. But in a place like Live Bay, you didn't run into this sort of girl.

I was positive Larissa was as entertained as me. Probably not as fascinated, but fucking entertained. Larissa was giving me the "be good" glare every time she came over to get our drinks.

She was my aunt, but she was only a couple of years older than me. We'd grown up more like cousins. She had lived with us for a time, but I was too young to remember.

It had taken some acting to pretend I wasn't as drunk as I actually was to get her to give me another whiskey.

Finally, I reached over and picked up one of the potato skins and held it to her little pink perfect mouth. She frowned immediately. "Eat it with your hands. Try it. The grease gets on your fingers, but somehow that makes it all better."

I wasn't a junk food guy. I was a runner and very careful about the food I ate until I got drunk. Then I ate all the bad shit. However, Lila was keeping me from eating the greasy bar food. I was too enthralled with her to care about anything else.

She took a dainty bite, and then cover her mouth as she chewed, grinning as if she had done something completely wicked. Damn, that was hot. There was no way she was as perfect as I saw her. She had to have something wrong with her. I just couldn't see clearly through the drunken haze. I needed to tread carefully.

I tried to focus harder to see if her teeth were bucked or if there was a gap big enough for food to fit through. Maybe she had bad breath? Or was married? I began checking those for evidence of those intently.

"What are you doing?" she asked.

I wasn't about to tell her I was trying to focus enough to find her flaws. There had to be a reason I was the only guy in this bar hitting on her. If she was, in fact, as fucking perfect as my mind was telling me she was, then she should have several guys hovering around her. That was my first clue. I could ask Larissa, but then she'd stop giving me drinks, and possibly slap me across the face for being so shallow.

I went with the best excuse. "I was trying to figure out if you were married or engaged."

She laughed then. Out loud. A musical sound that made me feel nice all over. "Married? Why would you think I was married? And why were you studying my mouth like it was a science experiment? Was it going to tell you I was married?"

I wasn't very smooth. Maybe I should drink some water.

"Just checking to see if those green onions were sticking in your teeth. They always get in mine."

She laughed again. Damn, I liked that laugh. I liked that she thought my lie was funny.

"Thanks, I think. I assume I passed the inspection."

I nodded because she still looked perfect, and fuck me if it was the drunk goggles talking. If it was, I had a better imagination than I realized.

"Dance with me," I said standing up, thankful I didn't fall over. I could still balance. That was good.

"Drink this water first, Romeo," Larissa interrupted me. Her serious expression told me maybe I wasn't hiding my drunk that well. So, I took the glass and downed it.

She cut her eyes to Lila. "I'm trusting you," were her final words to me before she walked back to help other customers. It sucked when your aunt was the bartender at the only place in town that was worth going to. Well, it didn't always suck, but tonight it was getting in my way.

I smirked and blew it off. "Larissa is my aunt. You'll have to ignore her."

Lila's stunning eyes widened in surprise. "Oh. She looks so young."

"She is. Only a few years older than me. The story is long, full of intrigue and lies. Very daytime soap opera. I'll tell you all about it if you dance with me. I swear it's better than a romance novel." That much was true. Larissa's story was intense.

Lila looked down at her uneaten food. "I can't eat any more anyway. You were right they are delicious but heavy. I'm full." She stood up and gave me that smile that I hoped I remembered tomorrow.

I placed a hand on her lower back and led her out to the dance floor. Glancing at the table I had been at when she walked in, I saw Micah Falco and Jimmy Taylor give me the nod. They were both smiling. Either they were smiling because she was as smoking hot as I thought she was, or because they were going to harass me about this for years to come. I just didn't care anymore. And I was fucking thrilled Saffron's crazy ass wasn't here tonight to cause trouble. She'd ruin this just for the hell of it.

Even if I did forget fragments of tonight, Micah and Jimmy would surely give me a complete recap. Once we were on the packed dance floor, I pulled her to me and inhaled. Jesus, she smelled like heaven. She wasn't wearing some heavy perfume or body lotion. It was light and smelled like almonds or cinnamon. Fuck if I knew. It was just intoxicating. I pulled her closer and took a deep breath.

"I'm sure you hear this a lot, but you smell amazing."

She tilted her head back just enough to look up at me. "Thanks. And no, I don't actually."

That caused me to pause. Did she live in a convent? "How is that possible?"

She gave me a small shrug. "I don't get close to guys often." She hesitated, then she looked serious like she was unsure she should have said that. "I mean I didn't for a long time, but I do now. I'm different. It's time for a change."

A change? What was she a lesbian trying out the other side? I decided against asking that figuring if it was the case she might be offended. Didn't matter to me either way.

"What all does this change of yours consist of?" I asked her.

"Adventure."

Just that one word. Interesting. She had eaten her bar food with a knife and fork with her paper napkin in her lap and she wanted an adventure. I wasn't sure that was safe. She seemed too innocent for an adventure. Or maybe I was reading her completely wrong?

"What is this adventure?"

"I'm not sure yet. But I am on it now. Bars, random guys, bar food—that's all part of it."

"Am I the beginning of your adventure?"

She smiled and then nodded. "Yes, Eli, you are."

Chapter Four

♥ LILA KATE ♥

DANCING WITH ELI at this bar wasn't my first time to dance at a bar. I had once before while in college. A friend on the dance team had her twenty-first birthday party at the local haunt. I went. I danced. I left early and arrived home before midnight sober. But that was the old me.

"I think I'd like another drink," I told Eli after our dance.

He smiled as if I was amusing. "Anything in particular?"

I almost said a martini and stopped myself. "Whatever."

He chuckled and I watched as he held his hand up signaling a waitress who was carrying a tray of little shot glasses filled with Jell-O. She came over and he took two glasses off her tray. "Thanks."

Then he handed one to me.

"What's this?" I asked holding the cup of Jell-O in front of me.

"A Jell-O shot. It's even better than a bar drink. It's a club drink."

The club he was referring to was different than the club I had grown up in and I knew that. I figured why not. I tasted it slowly.

"It's a shot, Lila. Don't savor it. Just down it."

Not wanting to disappoint him or me, so I did as Eli said.

When I was done, I thought it tasted yummy like strawberry Jell-O.

"What did you think?"

"I liked it."

He handed me the shot glass he was holding. "I never was one to think a guy looked right doing a Jell-O shot. Take this one."

And I did.

I wasn't sure what liquor was in them, but my head felt lighter, and I felt happy. Eli took both cups, held his hand up again and placed them on the tray the waitress was carried over to us.

"Ready for another dance?" he asked.

I stepped back into his arms and we danced. This time I wasn't aware of anyone around us, and I wasn't concerned. I enjoyed myself. Moved by the music, I let go of my inhibitions. I laughed. I heard my own laughter and it felt right.

It wasn't until three dances later when Eli took a drink off a tray and drank it that I wondered what time it was. I should call my mom. I should call Nate.

Then I realized that was the old Lila Kate. This was the new one.

Our dancing continued. Our movements got sexier. The touching became more intense and my heart rate sped up a bit. I enjoyed being near Eli. I liked the way his hands slid over my hips and cupped my bottom. When my breasts brushed against his chest, the contact felt like electricity had pulsed through me. These feelings were all new things for me. I'd tried to feel this before. It had never happened. I was always so tense and unsure. But Eli was easy to trust, and the way he smiled could attract a nun.

His head lowered, and his breath was hot on my neck. I shivered as it tickled my ear. "Go somewhere with me."

I slowed our dance to a halt. This was it. My chance to do something truly wild. To break free of the old me. To become someone else. I needed this. I wanted this. I wanted Eli, and it had been awhile since there was a guy that attracted me. It wasn't just the shots either. I'd liked him before I started drinking.

"Okay," I answered loud enough that he could hear.

He bit softly on my earlobe. "I'll get your purse from Larissa."

I nodded and walked off the dance floor with him.

He got my purse from his aunt who he'd handed it to when we left the bar for the dance floor. Then he came straight to me. "Your car here?" he asked.

"Yes."

"I'm not sure either of us should drive just yet. Walk with me down the beach."

I had to agree. I wasn't sure I should get behind the wheel, and he had drunk more than I had. His hand slipped over mine then our fingers threaded. We walked in the moonlight across the road and down to the beach in silence. The music from Live Bay faded in the distance.

It was secluded and peaceful on the shore. I'd been on our beach many times at night. But never with a guy. Not like this. It was almost magical.

"You swim in the Gulf much? Or are you on the East Coast?"

"I'm on the west, and no. I enjoy the beauty but I don't get in it much."

"Where in Florida do you live?"

I wavered here, not sure what I should say. I wanted to leave that girl behind. Rosemary Beach was small but it was elite. Everyone knew that wealthy and famous people lived there. He'd wonder. He'd ask questions. I'd reverted to Lila Kate Carter in moments. I didn't want to be her again.

"A small little town. Nothing special."

He nodded. "Okay. I won't push."

I sighed. It sounded like I was keeping it from Eli because I didn't trust him. I was out here alone with him. That was trust right there. "It's not that. It's . . . I don't want to be her anymore. I want to be different. I want to be someone new."

"Adventure," he added.

"Yes."

He stopped as we came to a dark and secluded spot on the beach with nothing but the waves crashing to the right of us and tall sea grass to the left. Houses and condos had tapered off. He turned to me, and his hands took my waist. I would be lying if I said I didn't hold my breath. When his mouth met mine, I inhaled sharply. His lips were firm, yet they were tender. He knew exactly how to use them too. Our tongues danced as his hands moved down over my bottom then up under my top until both of his palms were cupping my breasts.

My breathing was already erratic when his thumbs brushed my nipples. However, when he lifted my shirt to remove it, I hesitated. I wasn't sure. I didn't know him. Could I do this? I lifted my eyes and looked up at his perfectly chiseled face. I decided this was the right time. A real adventure. And he was exactly who I wanted to experience it with.

I allowed Eli to remove my shirt. He stared a moment and let my shirt drop from his hand, then took my bra off and dropped it on top of my shirt. His expression was appreciative. I forgot to breathe again when Eli's head descended slowly to my chest, his mouth covered my nipple, and he began to suck. I held onto his head because my knees felt weak. He seemed to know exactly what I needed. He stopped to pull off his shirt. He laid it out on the sand then did the same with his jeans. I watched with fascination as his lean muscular body was now on display for me. Once he finished making a makeshift bed, he lowered his tall frame to rest on his clothes, and pulled me down on top of him.

I straddled him, my skirt hiking up my thighs and nothing separating us but his boxers and my panties. His hands threaded through my hair, and he held my head looking into my eyes. "You're fucking perfect, Lila. That seems impossible."

"I am so far from perfect."

He smiled and then his eyes went dark making me shiver. His eyes dropped to my bare chest. "I want to taste you."

I wanted to kiss him too. "Okay," I agreed.

In one swift movement, he rolled me underneath him and I could feel his rumpled clothes and sand beneath me. I was startled, but when my knees were put over his shoulders I realized what he had meant and my stomach flipped. I'd never done this. No guy had ever been that up close and personal with me. Nervous didn't even begin to describe it.

Then his tongue slid over the inside of my thigh and I froze. I don't know if it was anticipation or fear for what was to come next. Those lips that knew how to move against mine began working the same magic between my legs. With every swipe of his tongue and carefully placed kiss I cried out, trembled, and began to beg. This was the most erotic, exciting moment of my life. I never wanted it to end. Ever.

Chapter Five

~ELI HARDY~

WATER. I HADN'T drunk enough fucking water. I lie in bed with my head pounding afraid to open my eyes. This was going to be one hell of a hangover. I never drank like I did last night, and this was why. I hated feeling like shit.

Wait . . . that smell. I inhaled again. The scent was still there. Holy shit. I remembered that smell. Almond and cinnamon and maybe vanilla. It sounded like a sugar cookie but that wasn't what I was smelling. It was her.

I opened my eyes and looked around my bed. No. Just me. I was clothed. But Lila's smell. I held my arm up to my nose and sniffed. Yes. That was her. But how? From dancing? We'd ate the potato skins I would have to run off today. Then we danced. Then . . . hell if I knew. I couldn't remember shit.

Had I left her there? Just walked out? I didn't even know her last name. But then the perfect cookie smelling girl in my drunken memories was probably much less perfect than I had thought. I'd been drunk after all. When had any man made a wise decision drunk? Never.

My phone rang, and I covered it with my other pillow to drown out the annoying sound. Moaning, I sat up and stretched. Water and Tylenol. I needed both now. Even if the idea of standing sounded like hell.

The lights in the apartment were off which meant I hadn't been too drunk to remember to turn shit off. I just didn't remember coming back here at all. It was possible Larissa brought me home. That would explain how my truck keys were on the kitchen bar and I was waking up alive.

I took a glass out of the cabinet and filled it with tap water then popped open the bottle of Tylenol rarely used in my drawer. Once both were consumed, I toasted some bread and grabbed an apple then went to sit in the living room with more water. I wanted coffee, but I wasn't going to touch that after the harm I'd done to my body last night.

Leaning back on the sofa I let out another miserable groan. Why had I let myself get so damn drunk? It wasn't like I had a lot to be upset over. My job was stable. I was healthy. I had friends. My best friend was engaged, and that sucked, but I was getting used to it. But damned if I hadn't needed an escape last night.

The toast was all I could stomach. I finished both pieces and left the apple on the table beside me. I couldn't eat any more. That would have to suffice for now. Once I felt like a human, I would go for a run. Then get brave enough to call Larissa and ask what I did last night.

Other than the fact I had gotten a little drunk. Or a lot drunk. Not me at all. But for the time it had felt nice. I'd enjoyed Lila. I was on a no women streak, but I only flirted and danced with her. Nothing more. Besides she was on her way to find an adventure. I remembered that. It made me smile. That girl and her adventure sounded very Alice in Wonderland-like.

I would have to ask Larissa if she'd been that stunningly perfect or if it had been my drunken state. Just so I could remember her correctly. Then maybe it was best I kept my memories untouched by reality. I hadn't woken up in bed with her or married. That was a success.

I heard the muffled sound of my phone ringing again. Someone was persistent this morning. Yawning then wincing from the pain in my head, I got up from my comfortable spot and went to get my phone from under the pillow.

Only one side of my bed was messed up. Another positive thing. Or was it? Her smell was still on me, and the way she'd felt in my arms when we danced—it might not have been a bad thing if I'd woken up with her curled up beside me.

I paused and let my imagination take over for a moment. I could see her brown hair and pretty eyes smiling at me. That sweet smell that I could fucking soak in. Eventually, she'd speak and start talking about our wedding and our children and how she would need space in my closet and a panty drawer in my dresser. *Stop. Run.* That was the reason I was swearing off women for a while. They all wanted to handcuff you and take you to the alter. Not that I didn't want to get married one day. I did. But not right now. And not until I was hit by a woman that I couldn't live without.

So far, that hadn't happened.

Picking up my phone I saw Bliss York's name. She'd be Bliss Finlay in six months' time. She was my best friend who I'd been in love with most my life. I was happy for her. She'd faced death and won. She deserved this. I just had always imagined it would be with me. Nate Finlay had come into our world and changed it all.

I still loved her. But I'd accepted she loved someone else, and I was beginning to think she was the reason I feared women wanting more. I had loved Bliss for as long as I could remember. How was I ever going to love someone else like that? It scared me to get too close because in the end, it would hurt them. What if Bliss was still it for me? What if they couldn't take her place or make me forget? So far, that hadn't happened.

It wasn't like I ever thought she loved me back. At least not that way. She'd never acted like she loved me anymore than a friend. It was something I had harbored myself. Our parents were close. My mother and her father had grown up as best friends too. We had been in each other's cribs since we were born. To Bliss, I was like one of her brothers. Except my future didn't include jail.

Her brothers were hell raisers.

I debated calling her back. I wasn't in the mood to be happy and listen to her happy shit. My head was still pounding. Then a text lit up my screen. *Made a big breakfast. Come eat.*

That kind of stuff was annoying. Bliss liked when I visited them. What it did was make me see them be all domestic and happy. I went. Because I couldn't remember a time in my life I didn't do whatever I could to see Bliss smile. Slowly though, that need was diminishing. She had Nate to make her smile. I didn't want that job anymore. Not if I wasn't going to be coming home to her at night. My plans for my future had always included her. Not now. Not that way at least.

Lila's idea of leaving town didn't sound so bad. Take off and reinvent yourself. Find a new way. The problem was I had a job, an apartment, and a life here that I couldn't just run from. I wasn't sure how she was funding her adventure, but I didn't have the funds for that.

I wanted to respond to the text *Thanks, but I've got plans.* Or *Thanks, but I'm busy.* That would be breaking loose from making her happy. That would be what a real man would do. Instead, I replied, *Just got up. Let me shower. Then I'll head over.*

Dropping my phone on my bed, I growled at my weakness. It was like I needed to be nice. To do the right thing. Dammit, I hated that about myself. The last thing I wanted to do this morning was head to their house and eat with them. Why couldn't they eat alone?

My phone dinged again. *Great. Nate's friend is here visiting. I want you to meet her.*

Shit. This was a hookup. And why did Nate have a female friend visiting them?

Her? I texted back.

Yes. We will wait on you to eat.

I wanted to ask more questions, like if anyone else was invited. Because I didn't need a fucking hookup. Bliss knew me better than that. I was on a "no women" hiatus. She also knew that. This had better only be an honest meet the friend thing. I wondered if Nate's "friend" was secretly in love with him. Hell, we may end up having a lot in common after all.

Chapter Six

♥ LILA KATE ♥

I STOOD IN the warm shower longer than necessary. I still had some sand stuck to me in places I've never had before. I closed my eyes and tried not to judge myself too harshly. I had been doing what I set out to do. Eli was a nice guy. He was sweet and gentle. And when he'd pulled a condom out of his pocket I had been extremely grateful.

The words he'd said while he made love to me were dirty, but they had made me crazy. Of course, he hadn't called it making love. He'd used the word fuck a lot. I touched the tenderness between my legs and smiled then. I had been wild. I'd had a one night stand. Me. Lila Kate Carter had been a harlot! That made me giggle.

Even through haze of the warm shower, I could smell bacon and cinnamon. Whatever Bliss was cooking was making my stomach growl with anticipation. After all the dancing, the walking then the best sexual experience I'd ever had, I was ravenous.

Luckily, the sex had sobered me up enough to drive here last night. But I still didn't think Eli was ready to drive. I left him with Larissa in the parking lot when we had walked back. He'd kissed me like a man hungry for more. I had soaked it all in, not wanting ever to forget that night.

He hadn't asked for my number, my last name, nothing. It had been just that for him too. A one night stand. It made me a little sad I wouldn't ever get to know more about him or see him again. Eli would always be my first experience as the new and improved Lila.

Reluctantly, I got out of the shower and dried my hair with a towel, then dressed in a pair of casual white linen shorts and a navy blue sleeveless top that was soft. I started to dry my hair with a hair dryer and stopped. The old Lila Kate would get presentable before going to breakfast. The new Lila would head there with wet hair and bare feet. If I were at home, I'd eat my breakfast like this. Why not here? They didn't expect me to be fixed up.

I hung up my towel because although I was more laid back now, I wasn't rude. Then I headed toward the smell of the food. The house that Nate and Bliss lived in was elegant, large, and what I'd expect Nate Finlay to purchase for him and his future wife. It sat on the water just like the house he'd grown up in. It wasn't anything as elaborate as his parents' home but it was still very impressive. Bigger than my home for sure.

Just as I stepped into the kitchen, the doorbell rang. Bliss spun around and smiled brightly when she saw me. "Good morning, I'm sorry I was asleep when you got here last night. There are different coffees to choose from right there," Bliss said as she pointed at a neatly organized pile of coffee K-cup pods. "Take your pick. There's even some tea or hot cocoa K-cups if you don't want coffee. Just help yourself. I will be right back. That's our other breakfast guest," she said as she left the room to answer the door.

I tried not to think about sitting down with other people for a fancy breakfast with wet hair and bare feet. It was ridiculous to worry about that. I looked at the coffee and tea choices. I liked tea but I preferred a nice bag to steep in hot water—not tea out of a little plastic pod. I picked out a breakfast blend coffee and made my cup.

"Morning party animal," Nate's voice startled me. I'd been staring at my cup as it filled with coffee, my thoughts still on last night.

I felt my cheeks heat. Nate was awake when I came in with messy hair, sand sticking to me, and smelling like a bar. He'd laughed. Loudly. Then told me he lied to my mother and told her I was so tired when I got here I fell asleep and that I'd call her in the morning. At the time, I was still floating on the memories of my wild evening. I'd thanked him, apologized for being late, and then went to clean myself up and get to bed.

"Good morning," I said feeling more embarrassed about my arrival last night. I was thankful that Bliss had been sleeping.

"Hungover?" he asked.

I shook my head. "No, I didn't drink enough for that."

He smirked. "Alrighty. Well, Bliss has made one of her feasts. She also invited her best friend over. It may be a setup—I can't decide. I'm warning you now. The guy coming over is in love with her. She doesn't believe that. But I see it. Just smile and we will get through breakfast."

Setup? I suddenly lost my appetite. "I don't need a setup. I'm leaving in a few days."

Nate shrugged. "I know. But you can't tell Bliss that. She says it's not. I just think deep down it may be. She just isn't admitting it. She worries about him. Either way, the woman can cook. You'll enjoy it. She's also fucking precious and hard not to love. You'll see. I can't blame the guy."

I nodded. "Okay." What else could I say?

"Here, grab the tray there with the fancy-ass muffins on

them. I'll grab the casserole," Nate said. "She'll want it all on the table before we eat."

I followed behind him with the food. "By the way Lila, I'm proud of you. Leaving isn't easy."

I smiled. I didn't need Nate Finlay to be proud of me. But it was nice to hear someone tell me they were. "It was easy for you."

"Yeah, but for you . . . it's a big deal. I'm impressed. Your mom's worried sick, but you're a woman now."

I started to say something else, but the words vanished. I stopped walking. Because as I stood there with my damp hair, bare feet, and hands full with a tray of muffins, my first adventure came walking into the room. Bliss York was walking in with Eli. My Eli.

Oh, my God.

He was talking to Bliss and hadn't looked our way. I couldn't move. I was stuck there. Nate's words were running through my head, taunting me. Eli was Bliss's best friend that was in love with her? Of all the guys at that bar, this had to be the one to approach me. This had to be the one that made my heart flutter and made me want to be near him.

I wasn't sure if I should move and draw attention to myself. Would he tell them? Would he say my name like he knew me? Or would he pretend like last night didn't happen?

"You look rough this morning. Wild night?" Nate said, and at that moment Eli turned his head in our direction. Our gazes locked. He squinted as if I were a blurry image and he needed to focus to see me.

"Eli this is Lila Kate. She's Nate's friend. They've known each other their entire life just like we have. Lila Kate this is Eli. He's normally more verbal, but he seems to be a bit hungover," Bliss said with amusement in her tone.

I waited. I wasn't sure what we were going to do here. My guess was we weren't going to share with these two we'd had sex on the beach. At least I hoped he wouldn't.

"We've met," he said a smile finally touching his face. The smile I remembered from last night. "At least I think we did. I drank more than I should have last night so it's all a little fuzzy, but you're the girl from the bar last night. Live Bay? I talked you into eating the potato skins?"

He sounded incredibly convincing. I went with it. "Yes. That was me," I replied.

"So that's where you were last night," Nate said. His voice sounded surprised and almost impressed. "Explains a lot."

I didn't look at him. I also stopped looking at Eli. Instead, I decided to study the food on the table. This was me being awkward. I was good at awkward. I was a pro.

"Those potato skins are delicious," Bliss said with pleasure in her voice. "I'm so happy you two met last night. Nate and I will get the rest of the food in here. Y'all get comfortable. We will be right back."

Bliss was a little too happy about this. I realized that this might have been a setup after all and her reaction made it clear she thinks we made it easier by meeting last night. Once they were out of the room, I chanced a glance at Eli. He was still studying me.

"My memory was correct. I'm a little surprised. I thought for sure it was the alcohol vision making you appear as perfect and prim as you are. I see that it wasn't."

I blushed and fidgeted with my hands. That was nice of him to say. I think?

"If I'd known you were exactly what I thought I was seeing I'd have figured out a way to get you to leave with me. But I'd had too many whiskeys to make any smooth moves. I regret that now."

There was a friendly tease to his voice. But that wasn't what made me pause. It was what he'd said. He would "have figured out a way to get me to leave with" him. As in, I didn't leave with him. Surely he was just saying that in case Bliss and Nate could hear us. He wasn't that drunk. Was he?

"Oh," I replied needing to say something.

"The dancing was nice. Real nice," his voice lowered. "I could still smell you on my skin when I woke up this morning."

Was he talking figuratively or in code? I glanced back at the door, and neither Bliss or Nate were anywhere in sight. This was confusing.

Before I had to think of something to say to him Nate appeared with a fruit tray. "If you two aren't planning on hooking up, just tell her. She'll drive us all crazy with the matchmaking if you don't get to the point."

Nate was blunt. I'd always liked that about him until now. Right now, it was not the time. He didn't know that though. Thank goodness he didn't know what had happened.

"Although you look like shit and this one got in late looking a little messy. So, I have my suspicions, but I won't pry. Just keep it to yourselves," Nate said with finality. Then he waved his hands at the table. "Y'all sit. I'm starving."

I took the chair closest to me. Nate sat at the end near the door that led toward the kitchen. Eli sat across from me. His gaze was serious at times while he looked at me like he was trying to remember something. I was afraid that something was what happened after we left the bar. The more he stared with that confused frown the more convinced I was he didn't remember the beach at all. Sex with me had been that forgettable. My happy thoughts this morning were gone.

"I did savory and sweet. Eli, I have some healthy for you," Bliss looked at me. "He may have talked you into the potato skins last night, but normally he eats like a health nut. It can be annoying."

I forced a smile as if I cared.

Chapter Seven

~Eli Hardy~

S HE HADN'T BEEN a dream. But the flirty girl from last night with the shy smiles and gazes was gone. This one was tense and obviously uncomfortable with the situation. She even seemed upset. I for one thought I was still dreaming when I walked in and saw her there. All fresh faced with hair damp from the shower looking as damn perfect as I remembered.

I tried to get her to look at me, but she kept focusing on her food that she barely touched and only looked up to speak if asked a question by Nate or Bliss. It was becoming obvious to everyone that she didn't want to be at this table with me. Bliss had even begun giving me questioning looks like I'd done something wrong. Hell, I was drunk last night. I just remember her eating the potato skins with a fork and how good she felt in my arms while we danced, and then things went black. The one time my never drinking much has kicked me in the ass. I decided to get drunk, and my low tolerance knocked me out.

I needed to call Larissa when I got home. Ask her about it. She'd know. She knew it all working behind that bar.

"Where are you headed next, Lila Kate?" Bliss asked too cheerfully. I also noticed they were calling her Lila Kate. Not just Lila. She'd introduced herself as Lila. That I was sure of. Lila Kate was cute but sounded childish. Was that annoying her? Because it was bugging me. I was ready to correct Bliss.

"I'm not positive. I was going to study a map today. Make a decision. I have a few ideas. Friends I'd like to visit."

So, this adventure she'd spoken of hadn't been something I dreamed up.

"You're traveling alone?" I asked. I still didn't think that was a good idea.

She barely glanced at me and gave a tight nod. "Yes."

"Is that safe?" I asked.

She went very stiff. Her shoulders went back, and her head tilted suddenly in a very regal pose. Interesting. She looked like a Kennedy as she answered, "Yes."

"Lila Kate can pull a pistol and not miss under pressure. She's unassuming but lethal," Nate said with a crooked grin.

"You carry a gun?" I asked incredulously. I didn't even carry a gun, and I was a male in Alabama.

She gave a dainty lift of her left shoulder. "Of course."

"You must have brothers like Bliss," I offered thinking that had to be the only excuse.

"No. I'm the only child."

"My mother gave her lessons. Harlow, Lila's mother, was nervous when Lila Kate started driving. So my mom offered to teach her how to handle a gun," Nate added.

I looked at Nate. "Your mom carries a gun too?"

Nate chuckled. "Oh, yes. My mother is feminine, beautiful, and a complete badass."

Bliss laughed with him. "Yes, she is," she agreed.

"Story goes, my mom's first night in Rosemary Beach she

pulled her gun on Lila Kate's dad. Scared the shit out of him," Nate was smiling as he said it.

That brought a small tug at the corners of Lila's mouth. She liked the story too. I watched hoping she'd smile that bright smile from last night where her eyes lit up. But it never came.

Bliss and Nate began laughing over his first meal at her parents' house when one of her brothers brought a gun out to threaten Nate. I listened to them talk, but my attention stayed on Lila. Once she finished her meal, she told Bliss how delicious it was and that she would clean the kitchen. She then excused herself to make a couple of phone calls. One was an important call to her mother.

After she'd left the room, Bliss glared at me. "What did you do to her?" she whispered.

I shrugged innocently. "I didn't do anything. I swear. We ate, drank and danced a couple of dances. That was it."

Bliss didn't look convinced. "She was quiet and nervous. Very uncomfortable."

"That's just Lila Kate. She's not a big talker. She doesn't draw attention to herself. She listens but rarely joins in. You'll get used to it," Nate explained. But I disagreed with him. The girl from last night hadn't been like that. Something had been wrong this morning. I just didn't know what.

"I want her to enjoy her stay here," Bliss said her voice sounding sad.

"She will, baby. I swear Lila Kate is just quiet. I've known her my entire life, and that's just her."

Bliss sighed then nodded. "Okay. Well, it's obvious she doesn't care for you," she said looking back at me. "Maybe I could take her shopping and invite Crimson instead. I bet she'd like your sister."

This was starting to annoy me.

Nate gave Bliss a smile that said he adored her and wished

they were alone. Normally, that made me uncomfortable or nauseous, but right now I couldn't seem to care. I needed to know why I'd pissed off Lila. I didn't like Bliss being frustrated with me either. Or let down.

"If you're finished eating you'd better go. So she'll feel more comfortable coming out here," Bliss said with an apologetic frown.

I was done. I needed to talk to Larissa anyway.

"Yeah, I'm finished. Thanks for breakfast," I said although I hadn't wanted to eat in the first place. So now my stomach felt even worse. "It was delicious." I stood and looked at Nate. "I didn't mean to make her uncomfortable. Last night I thought we got along fine."

"No worries. Seriously, that was typical Lila Kate. Bliss just doesn't know her yet. She'll get used to it."

Again, I disagreed and felt like maybe Nate didn't know her that well. I'd seen a much different girl last night . . . didn't I? Was that all an illusion from the drinking? Had I thought she was different because I'd been so sloppy drunk?

But damn if I could make up that smile and laugh. That had been real. I know it had.

"Okay, well, thanks for having me," I said again and then headed for the door. I wanted to find Lila and talk to her alone. But with these two in the house that wasn't going to happen. I could just hope I found her again before she took off on her trip.

Closing the door behind me, I walked out to my truck. Before I got in, I paused and glanced up at the windows. I'm not sure why, but I had sensed her. Sure enough, there Lila stood watching me in the window to the left looking down. She had her arms crossed over her chest defensively, and there was hurt in her eyes I could see from all the way out here. That was going to bother me.

I waited there. Staring back at Lila. Wishing she'd come out here but knowing she wouldn't. Finally, the curtain swung back, and she was gone. I didn't leave right away. I waited a moment to see if she was gone or just hiding from me. When nothing happened I finally climbed into my truck and left. I needed to some answers.

Chapter Eight

♥ LILA KATE ♥

I WATCHED THROUGH the curtains until he left. Our encounter shouldn't be a big deal. I'd thought he was a one-night stand. A guy I'd never see again. Just because he was too drunk to remember me that well or that we'd had sex—which was blatantly obvious—shouldn't bother me. Besides, I'd be leaving here in a couple of days. It wasn't like I was going to see him again.

He was in love with Bliss. I imagined most guys were in love with Bliss. She was the kind of girl guys fell in love with. Beautiful, smart, outgoing, confident, and still kind.

I had watched Nate Finlay date so many females over the years I'd lost count. Even when he was engaged, I hadn't seen him look at a woman like he did Bliss.

It still stung. I hadn't been a wild one-night stand. I had been a drunken rebound. If I had truly had sex with a guy I would never see again, then I wouldn't have known exactly what it had been for him. What I did know were the things he had said to me, the way he'd made me feel desirable and sexy had all been crap. He had just been drunk, and apparently a master with words while intoxicated.

I couldn't hate him for that. I could, however, keep my distance. That was best. I didn't think Bliss would be scheduling any meals with him again while I was here. She'd hoped for something with that setup. I guess deep down Bliss knew her best friend was in love with her and was trying to move his attention elsewhere.

A knock on the door to the bedroom I was staying in interrupted my thoughts. That would be Bliss coming to check on me. To see if I wanted to do something. I was expecting that.

"Come in," I called turning to face her as she entered the room.

Her smile was genuine. She was the sort of person that you saw the kindness in their eyes. I didn't know many people like that back home. At least, not females. If they weren't close friends or family, they were rather vicious. A curse that came with growing up among the elite.

"I hope I didn't interrupt. I know you needed to call your mother."

I still needed to do that. "No, not at all."

She looked relieved. "I thought maybe we could do some shopping, have lunch at Nate's grandfather's place, and visit a few friends of mine. All girls this time," she blushed as she said the last part. I was glad we weren't going to recap that breakfast and my night with Nate. Bliss wasn't the nosey type. I liked that about her, too.

"Okay, yes, that sounds nice. I don't want to keep you from anything, though. Don't feel as if you need to entertain me."

Bliss beamed at me then. "When Nate said you were coming to visit I took off work. I wanted to have plenty of time to show you around."

If I lived here, I think Bliss and I could be good friends. But I wouldn't live anywhere for a long time. This was just my first stop.

"Thank you, that's very thoughtful of you. I felt as if I sprung this on you and Nate. It was very last-minute planning."

Bliss's eyes seemed to understand more than I had told her. "I had to get away too once. I didn't get far, but it was enough. Sometimes space from what we know is needed."

I simply nodded. Because she was correct. Although there was much more to mine. I didn't imagine she needed to recreate herself. Find a new Bliss. She seemed perfect as she was. My mother was perfect like her. My father was outgoing and handsome. Everyone loved being around him. How had I turned out so . . . so . . . different?

I couldn't blame them. They'd do anything to give me a full life. We were a close family. They'd been excellent role models. But I was the odd little duckling. I preferred books and solitude. I was proper and polite. That I did blame on my mother. However, my mother appeared dainty and elegant when she did things like eat potato skins with flatware.

"I'm ready whenever you are. Just come on down when you're ready to leave."

I wasn't about to have her waiting for me downstairs. That was rude. And although I was trying to be less of a rule follower and more carefree I wouldn't be rude.

"Let me brush my hair and find some shoes, then I'll be ready."

She seemed pleased with that, then left the room closing the door behind her. Nate's mother, Blaire, had come over for coffee the morning after Nate had brought Bliss for a visit to tell us all about her. She'd been thrilled for Nate. She loved Bliss, and she had been right. Everything she raved about. The dinner party Blaire held at her house the last night of their stay I had met Bliss. I'd even spoken to her a few moments, but that was all. She'd been whisked off by Ophelia, Nate's sister, to meet other guests. I was surprised Nate even allowed his mother to plan an event like that.

He seemed protective of Bliss.

But then he had never really been able to control his mother. If he tried to say no to her about something, his father would step in. Bliss seemed to enjoy herself that night though. It had been no problem at all that she was cast into a large, close-knit bunch.

I went into the private bathroom that was connected to my room and finished drying my hair with the dryer. Then added some lip gloss. I thought about doing more but didn't. I left the bathroom to find some sandals and slipped them on. After a quick inspection, I put on a pair of small silver hoop earrings and a few of my favorite bangle bracelets.

Satisfied, I left the room and went to find Bliss. The house was lovely inside. Bliss had obviously done some decorating of her own. It had a homey feel even if it had wide hallways, tall ceilings, elaborate crown molding and chandeliers in most rooms. Somehow, she'd given it a touch of comfort. I respected that.

When I arrived at the foot of the stairs, Bliss was walking out of a backroom with a smile on her face that was somewhat dreamy. I didn't need to know she had been in there with Nate. I'd seen that look on my mother's face many times. I guess some people did get fairy tales. Even if they had to live through tragedy first.

I had no dramatic tragedy in my life. I had nothing. My life roadmap was bare. No excitement, just the same thing. Every day. I should be thankful for that I guess. Tragedy wasn't exactly something to wish for.

"Oh, you're ready. That was fast. Let me grab my purse and we'll go." Her tone chipper and her cheeks a little flushed.

"No rush," I said hoping I hadn't been interrupting anything. Having me stay here during the newness of their engagement was probably difficult for them. I hadn't considered that. I should spend some time tonight figuring out my next stop and get moving along. So far, there was nothing keeping me here in Sea Breeze.

Chapter Nine

~ELI HARDY~

I DIDN'T CALL Larissa. I knew she'd be awake. Jilly, her daughter, was three and she woke up with the sun, even after Larissa worked late nights. She refused to leave her with a sitter until the next morning. She sent the sitter home when she got there, and she was Mom until she had to work again. Sometimes I wondered if she had superhuman powers.

I rang the bell, and heard sounds of kid's shows coming from inside. Then I heard Jilly call out, "Someone is here!"

The kid was cute. It was a shame her dad was missing out on her life. The guy had been a complete jerk. I'd told Larissa that when she was dating him. When he left, though, I didn't say I told you so. That was cold, and I knew Larissa was hurt enough. She was a great mother. She never needed his sorry ass. Neither did Jilly. It was his loss.

The door opened and Larissa stood there with her hair in a messy knot on top of her head and a cup of coffee in her hand. She looked wide awake. Guess getting up at six gives you plenty of time to drink the coffee.

"Surprise, surprise, if it isn't the drunk Romeo," she said with a roll of her eyes. She turned around leaving the door open and walked back into the living area. Jilly was there playing with her toys and watching some show where a little girl was a toy doctor—or it looked like that anyway.

Larissa walked over and sat down on the sofa.

"Eli!" Jilly cried out with glee when a commercial came on. She ran over to hug my leg. I bent down and picked her up.

"Hey, squirt," I said then kissed her head.

"Hey," she replied giggling and curled against me. Then just as quickly, she squirmed to get down and went back to her toys.

"Want to know how you got home?" Larissa asked.

I wanted to know more than that.

"Or what happened after our third dance," I said.

Her eyes went wide. Then she burst out laughing. "You're kidding me, right? You weren't that bad off!"

"It wasn't my best night. Started out being frustrated with life. Drinking away the shit things had turned out with Micah and Jimmy. Then I saw her walk in and acted. Thought the no-women rule was dumb and moved over there. I regret it now. Trust me. My head is still pounding."

Larissa was curled up on the sofa with her cup looking amused. "Well, she was one you wouldn't want to forget. Beautiful, but so proper it was funny. You were taken with her."

I knew all that. "Tell me what I don't remember. Not a recap of what I do."

Larissa sighed. "Well, okay. You danced a lot more than three dances. Then you left. You dropped your keys off with me because I insisted. You told me y'all were going for a walk on the beach. You were gone two hours. Then you came back when I was walking out after closing. I drove you home then had Micha drop your truck off. That's it."

That's it? "We left to go walking?"

She nodded. "Yep. That's it. She got in her Land Rover and drove away. That was it. Shame, too. She was one you'd want to keep. But her tag was a Florida one. She's not from around here."

I leaned my head back to rest on the chair and closed my eyes tightly in frustration. "Rosemary Beach, Florida to be exact. Want to know how I know that? Because I had breakfast with her this morning at Bliss and Nate's. She's Nate's friend. Passing through on this road trip adventure she's on. She owns a gun, too."

"No way!" Larissa said sounding excited. I didn't lift my head to look at her. "Oh, my God! You just walk into breakfast this morning not knowing, didn't you? Does Bliss know about last night?"

She was acting like this was a book and she needed to know the next chapter. I sighed. "No, I didn't know. Walked right in and 'bam' there she was. I told them we had met last night. That's all. She barely spoke to me or looked at me. I need to know what I did to make her act that way," I looked up then. "And she was as damn perfect as I thought she was when I was drunk. How is that? I thought she'd have some terrible flaw that my drunken vision was missing. But nothing. Just like I remembered."

Larissa giggled. "This is epic. Damn, I mean dang," she quickly corrected herself then looked to see if Jilly had been paying attention. Jilly had already been kicked out of daycare for cursing. It was frowned upon to tell the teacher you didn't want to take a fucking nap. It was cause for dismissal. Larissa was working on cleaning up her three-year-old's language.

"The killer was I think Bliss was trying to set us up."

Larissa smiled over her cup. "She was a little late for that."

"Yeah, and Lila—who they called Lila Kate—she didn't say much at all. Made it real clear she hadn't enjoyed the night before nor did she like having breakfast with me."

"You mean she dropped the polite, proper thing?"

"Oh, no. She had that going on. She just didn't speak to me unless forced."

"Ouch."

Ouch wasn't what I was thinking. More like what the hell did I do?

"So you have no idea what we did when we walked? Where we went?"

"I was working—you know my job? Serving drinks?" Her sarcasm wasn't lost on me.

"Maybe I can get her alone, and we can talk?"

"She staying in town that long?"

That part sucked. "No."

Larissa shrugged. "Then let it go."

If only I could. I didn't want to let it go, and I didn't want to let her go. Even if it was obvious I'd have to do both.

I gave Jilly another hug, but she was more interested in the dump truck that the little girl was fixing on television. I thanked Larissa and headed for the door.

"Please tell me if you see her again," Larissa called out. "I gotta know what happens next."

I rolled my eyes and closed the door behind me. That gave me a little more info, but now that I knew I left with her, I wanted to talk to her. What happened in those two hours had to do with why Lila didn't like me today. If I'd crossed a line or something I needed to know. Apologize. Shit. Do something!

Chapter Ten

~CRUZ KERRINGTON~

WHEN MY DAD calls me into his office, it is never a good thing. When he wakes me up at six in the motherfucking morning to inform me we have a tee time at six-thirty when he knows I hate golf, it's even worse. Golfing with Woods Kerrington meant he was going to talk to me. For eighteen goddamn holes.

My mother was awake with a cup of tea in her hands looking at her computer screen while standing at the bar when I walked into the kitchen. She lowered her cup and smiled. "You look bright and chipper this morning," she said sarcastically.

"Ugh," I grunted and went to make coffee from the machine. I hated the nasty shit, but I drank it when I was forced to get out of my bed before the damn sun.

"There's no hot cocoa in there. Zander drank it all. I need to go to the grocery store today."

"Coffee works," I muttered.

She had the nerve to chuckle. My mother wasn't soft and sweet. She hadn't been given a daughter. She'd been given three sons, and she held her own with us. As dainty as she looked she could scare the shit out of you if she snapped. Needless to say, none of us ran over our mom.

"Want a muffin? I made some fresh yesterday. Had to use up the blueberries before they went bad."

That made this morning a little better. But only a little. "Yes, please," I said wondering how I'd missed those when I got in last night. I normally could tell by the smell of the place when I got home if mom had been baking. I'd proceed to case the place for whatever she'd made.

She placed a plate in front of me with two muffins on it. "He just wants to spend time with you," she was trying to reassure me.

"Then why can't we spend time doing something I enjoy too. At a much later hour?" I grumbled.

"Because he has a job and it's time you took your own job more seriously."

My own. Meaning working under my father at the club. Going to meetings and learning the ropes. I had one more year of college then it all got real. I wanted to make my year last because my future didn't sound that exciting.

"Whatever," I replied before taking a bite. I braced myself to get slapped on the back of the head for that one word. It didn't happen, though. Instead, Dad walked in dressed and looking happy to be awake.

"Take that to go. We need to leave," he told me then went to kiss Mom. "If Zander isn't up by eight call me. I told him yesterday that he was in charge of cutting the grass today."

We didn't have much grass. The backyard was the beach. But cutting the grass didn't just mean cutting the grass. It meant doing all the other yard shit that he wanted done. You'd think we could hire a damn landscaper, but no. Dad said he had three sons he wasn't paying to get shit done that we could do.

"I'll get him up if he doesn't," mom said with a smug smile. That would involve ice. I know. She'd tossed some in bed with me before when I wouldn't budge.

Dad chuckled. "For his sake, I hope he gets up."

I took my second muffin and cup of coffee and headed for the door.

"Y'all have fun," Mom called out. As if that was possible.

Dad followed me out the door. "Get in my car. No need for you to drive."

That wasn't good. This meant he was going to keep me busy doing shit all day. I would be stuck there. Unless I used a club car to give me a ride home. But then he'd find out about that in seconds. Damn.

I went to his silver SUV and climbed into the passenger side. He got in, and we drove in silence. Thankfully. I drank my coffee which tasted like ass and ate the muffin. I wish Mom had given me three. The drive to the course was only minutes.

Just when I thought we were going to get out of this thing without any conversation, he paused before getting out of the vehicle. "I don't want to see my son fucking again on a security camera. Got that?"

Shit. I looked up at the clubhouse in front of us. I'd been drinking and forgot about the new security cameras inside. Wincing I climbed out and tossed back the rest of the coffee then left the cup behind.

"Your mother doesn't know. We aren't naive. We know you have a sex life. I just don't want to see it nor should our employees have to see it. That was embarrassing."

"Look, I forgot about the cameras. They're new. I was drinking and forgot."

He walked over to me and once he used to tower over me. I thought he was the tallest most powerful man in the world. Now we were eye to eye, and I was still fucking intimidated. His scowl didn't help ease me either. "You're not a kid anymore Cruz stop acting like one. Grow the fuck up. Now."

"Hot damn, I get to watch a good ole ass whoopin', and I don't have any popcorn," Grant Carter interrupted us. Dad continued to glare at me. He didn't stop because his friend had arrived.

"Morning, Grant," Dad said when he finally turned toward him and let me out of his threatening stare.

"I thought this was a friendly game this morning, but seeing as Junior is here and he hates golf, there's gonna be some excitement." Lila Kate's dad was rarely serious. He was the easiest going of my dad's close circle of friends. He was absolutely nothing like his uptight daughter.

Another car door slammed, and I moved my attention back to the parking lot. Rush Finlay was headed our way. Nate's dad was here too. What the hell? I looked back at my dad. "So this isn't some sick way to punish me?" I asked trying to figure out what was going on. If he wasn't going to ride my ass the next few hours then why were we here?

He cocked one eyebrow. "Oh no. It's punishment. For you. Not for me."

I realized then what was happening. Sneaky bastard. He planned on making my morning hell, and he'd have witnesses to make it more entertaining for him. Twisted man.

"Damn," I muttered, and he laughed then.

"Junior is in trouble," Grant told Rush.

"What did he do this time?"

"I had the unfortunate pleasure of watching my son fuck on camera." Dad gave me another dirty look.

"What?" Grant asked as his eyes went wide and he grinned ear to ear.

"The security cameras are new. I forgot," I said annoyed.

That got loud roars of laughter from both Grant and Rush. I stalked off ahead of them not wanting to listen to their jokes about this. I'd be mocked the entire eighteen holes.

"If that is all this is about, give the kid some slack. Isn't like you didn't have your share of pussy all around this place when you were his age. Hell, we all did." Grant was trying to take my side.

I glanced back to see what Dad would say.

"Your daughter is finished with college. She's left to find her path. She' doing something. Achieving something. She has goals. Ambition," he argued.

I was still stuck on the Lila Kate being gone bit. Where did she go? When did she leave? That didn't sound like Lila Kate at all. She was always up her parents' ass, doing what they wanted. I probably wouldn't have even fucked Chanel in that clubhouse and gotten caught on video if I hadn't been fighting off my attraction to Lila Kate. She messed with my head.

"She's a girl," was Grant's argument.

"That's not a good excuse," Rush added. "Phoenix is giving me hell. Girls aren't easy because they're girls. You just got fucking lucky because Lila Kate is exactly like her mother."

She had left town? And Grant was okay with this?

"Who went with her?" I asked trying to get back to what was important here.

"No one," was Grant's response.

"You just let her take off on her own?" I asked wondering if he'd lost his goddamn mind. He'd always been so overprotective.

"She's a grown woman. She' smart," was his defense

"She's at Nate and Bliss's right now," Rush added.

She was in Sea Breeze. She hadn't gotten far. "Where she going next?"

"She's not making sex videos in the clubhouse that's for damn sure," Dad drawled.

No. She'd never do that. Lila Kate wasn't that kind of girl. She also wasn't the kind to run off like this. Alone. But then she'd only gotten as far as Alabama. There was a good chance she'd come back home. Probably would. But . . . what if she didn't?

Chapter Eleven

♥ LILA KATE ♥

BLISS HAD NICE friends. But I didn't expect anything less. Today was fun. Enjoyable. I was glad I went. Now I needed to focus and decide where I would head next. Bliss had gone to the library where she worked to check on some things. I had decided to stay behind do some planning.

With the warm breeze, a towel to sit on, a notepad, and my iPhone for research, I sat down on the sand facing the water. My sunglasses shaded the sun, and it was peaceful. It felt like home. The part I loved. The warmth, sound of the waves, sand between my toes—things I had grown up with, and they'd always be a part of me. Wherever I ended up.

Making notes I was torn between going through Birmingham and visiting my friend or to keep going until I reached Nashville. Enjoy the city some then head on to the Smokey Mountains. It was either that or head west to Louisiana. I'd never been to New Orleans. That could be exciting. Traveling alone might not be very smart though.

"Mind if I interrupt?" the voice startled me, and I lifted my gaze to see Eli. I didn't think he'd come around again after this morning. At least I had hoped he wouldn't.

I wanted to say, "Yes, I do mind," but my manners wouldn't allow that. "I guess not."

He sank down beside me and sat on the sand. I didn't offer part of my towel. If he was going to make us do this, then he was going to get a sandy bottom.

"Breakfast was interesting," he began.

"Yes," I agreed.

He gave a soft chuckle. "You were the last person I was expecting. I was almost convinced I'd made you up in my mind."

That was ridiculous. "Get drunk like that often?" I asked just to be snarky.

"Never. Rarely. I'm sorry I was last night."

I bet he was sorry. "I can imagine."

He didn't say anything for a few moments. I studied the notebook in my hand.

"After the third dance . . . I, well, things go black. I remember nothing."

He was reminding me again how forgettable sex with me was. Great. Just what I wanted to discuss. I wasn't sure I believed that anyway. How did one just black out?

"You're not going to tell me what happened are you?" he said when I didn't respond.

I shrugged. "Nothing really. We walked. You stumbled a bit. I sobered up from my brief buzz, and then I left you with your aunt."

If he didn't remember it, then I wasn't going to give him a recap. It would be my secret.

"That's it?" he asked.

"That's it." I wasn't a liar. I avoided looking at him when I confirmed the lie because I knew my expression would give me away.

He sighed. "Then why do I get the feeling you hate me for something? The girl I remember from last night was friendlier."

Not going to answer that either. "You were drunk. You don't know if I was friendly or you just thought I was."

He smirked then. "You went for a walk on the beach with me. That's pretty damn friendly."

He had a point. I lifted my gaze to meet his, and was honest about what I was willing to be honest about. "I didn't think I'd ever see you again. Last night was my first time alone in a bar. It was my first time dancing with a stranger and drinking with one. I thought it was a memory I'd have, not something that I'd have to face at breakfast the next morning."

"I was surprised but happy to see you when I walked in. I'd regretted not getting your number. It was like I had a second chance."

A second chance? At what? He was in love with Bliss. He wasn't looking for someone else. "What were you hoping for exactly?"

He stared out at the water and gave a small lift of his shoulders. They were nice shoulders. Broad muscular shoulders. I was sure he got plenty of female attention. I was one of many. "I'd sworn off women for a while. Needed a break to clear my head. I was doing good too. I was focused. Getting things done. Running more. But then you walked in. I had been midsentence arguing over beer with my friends and I wasn't able to look away. That hasn't happened to me . . . in a long time."

That almost eased the sting from him forgetting we'd had sex. Almost. It did help.

"I leave here soon. Probably tomorrow. At the latest Monday."

He didn't look pleased about that. "I know. You've got that adventure to experience. But while you're here I'd like to be part of that adventure again. Maybe on your way back you might stop by and tell me how it all went. I just, I'd like to get to know you."

There were a lot of things I could say here. But the only thing that came out of my mouth was "Okay." I surprised myself with it.

The smile that crossed his chiseled face was nothing less than beautiful. He wasn't hard on the eyes that was for sure. And he may be in love with an almost married woman, but he was kind. He'd drunk too much, that didn't make him a jerk. I might have gotten completely drunk too if I loved someone who wouldn't ever feel the same way about me.

"What are your plans the rest of the evening?" he asked hopefully.

"I was going to decide my route, but that's it. I haven't spoken to Bliss and Nate. I don't know what they were planning on doing."

"It's Saturday night. Come back to Live Bay with me. I'd like to enjoy dancing with you sober. Then we can take a walk I do remember. I'll even buy you some bar food that you can eat with flatware. It'll amuse my friends and possibly charm them the way it did me."

He was very good with words. I was smiling despite everything else. "If Nate and Bliss don't have plans where I am involved, that would be nice. Let me check with them first."

He nodded to the notebook in my lap. "Is that your adventure?"

"Yes," I replied feeling a little embarrassed.

"Where is the next stop?"

"Nashville or New Orleans," I told him.

His eyebrows shot up. "New Orleans is dangerous for a girl traveling alone."

I'd already considered that. "I know. But what is an adventure without danger?"

"You want to live to tell about it."

I did. "I'm just thinking about it. The idea for this trip was to take off and not have a plan. But I like to know where I'm headed."

"I'm glad this was your first stop."

Maybe I was too.

Chapter Twelve

~ELI HARDY~

LILA TEXTED ME two hours later to tell me she was free tonight. I told her I'd pick her up at six and feed her, and then we'd go dancing. The front part of Live Bay was an actual restaurant with good food.

When I knocked on Bliss's door, it was the first time I didn't have a knot of regret or sorrow in my stomach. I'd never been honest with her about my feelings, but now it was too late. She was happy and in love. She'd never looked at me the way she did Nate.

Bliss opened the door and gave me her usual bright smile. "I was just about to call you. Come in. I need to talk to you about something."

She wasn't aware I was here to pick up Lila apparently. It was normal for me to stop by. Although not this frequently. "Okay," I said walking inside the door and scanning for any sign of Lila.

"I've been battling something," she laughed then. "Nate said I can do what I want. It's our wedding, and we don't believe in rules. I like that idea. No rules. Do it our way. You know?"

Bliss wanted to talk about her wedding? Seriously? I just

nodded.

"Do you want a drink? I've got bottled water in the fridge," she said sounding nervous.

"No. I'm good. Thanks," I replied studying her. She was fidgeting. Like she was worried about what she had to tell me.

"Okay, well, you want to sit? We don't have to stand here. I was just so anxious to talk to you after making my decision. Then you showed up, and I knew it was right."

She had no idea I was here to pick up Lila. I glanced around again to see if Lila had heard us, but she was nowhere in sight.

"We can stand. I'm not here to stay awhile," I told her.

She nodded. "Okay. Right. Okay," she was babbling now like she only did when she was nervous. What the hell was wrong with her? How could anything having to do with her wedding affect me?

"I want you to be my best man," she blurted.

"What?" came out of my mouth before I could stop myself.

"My best man. I don't need a maid of honor. Who would that be anyway? You're my best friend. So I should have a best man beside me. Not a maid of honor. You can't very well wear a dress," she laughed and then continued. "And you can't stand on Nate's side. You're my friend. His dad is going to be his best man. I just . . . I want you to be a part of my big day. You've been a part of all my big events in life. This should be no different. I won't have bridesmaids. We just decided on both having a best man. Then Jilly will be the flower girl of course. It sounds crazy, but it really isn't. It makes sense. You know?"

As much as I understood what she was saying I didn't think I could answer her. How was I supposed to stand up there and watch the girl I'd imagined I'd marry all my life marry someone else? When she had been sick, and I wasn't sure if she'd survive, I'd feared we'd never get a chance to live a life together. Getting married. Having kids. But she had beat cancer. And she was going to get married. Just not to me. But she wanted me to watch it up close and personal.

Motherfucker.

"Please, think about it. This will make my day complete. Having you up there just sounds right."

I had arrived without the knot in my stomach, but it was back now. Stronger than ever. "Yeah, okay, sure. I can do that."

I don't know how I managed to get the words out.

Bliss broke into a huge grin. "Thank you! This means the world to me."

It meant a form of hell for me. But I didn't say that. "Thanks for asking me."

"I need to tell Nate." She reached to pull her phone out, then her head snapped back up to look at me. "Wait, you came to see me. I took over the conversation. Were you just here to visit or did you need something?"

"Lila. I'm here to get Lila," I replied still reeling from what I'd been asked.

That brought back her smile. "So you're her plans for tonight. That's wonderful." And she meant it. Bliss wanted me to date someone. Find someone like she had. "Well, I'll just go on up to my room and read until Nate gets home. Y'all have fun," she said then gave me a quick hug. "Thanks again."

I didn't turn to watch her leave. I just stood there staring straight ahead. Letting this all sink in. I was so lost in my thoughts I didn't hear the footsteps until Lila had walked right past me and toward the liquor cabinet. I watched as she opened it, then glanced back at me over her shoulder. "Vodka or tequila?"

"Vodka," I replied.

"Good," she said as she grabbed the bottle of Grey Goose and turned back to me. "Come on." It sounded a lot like a command. I wasn't sure what she was doing, but I followed her out the door and down to the beach. She kept walking once we hit the sand. My longer strides caught up to her.

"What are we doing?" I finally asked.

"Walking until we're out of the view of the house," was her response. The vodka bottle still in her hand.

"Okay," that wasn't exactly an explanation, but I kept walking with her. Another quarter of a mile and we reached a large log that had long since washed up. It was sitting up high and away from the water.

She went to sit down, and I took the spot beside her. She opened the vodka and then took a long swig before handing it to me. "Here you need it more than I do," she said.

I took it and drank because she was right. I did. But she didn't know why.

"How long you been in love with her? Your whole life? Since you were kids or once you got older?"

Damn. "Is it that obvious?"

She shrugged. "No and yes. You look at her the way a man in love looks at a woman. But you don't do it all the time. You're careful. I just paid attention."

I handed the bottle back to her. She took it and sighed. "That's why I left," she said as took another drink. I was impressed. I didn't imagine Lila could drink straight vodka from the bottle. That didn't fit her at all. But she wasn't even wincing. I wondered if she would have been able to do the same with tequila. I realized what she said then. "You left because someone asked you to be in their wedding or because you love someone that doesn't feel the same?"

"I grew up with him. Been thrown together since we were kids. I always thought he was exciting and fun. He always made me laugh. And then one day he kissed me. I knew I was in love with him. But he didn't feel the same way."

Shit. "Nate?" I asked thinking I might just hate him after all.

She jerked her head to look at me, and then let out a loud laugh. "God no! That'd be like incest. I mean we aren't actually related, but it feels like it. Always has. Our dads were step brothers when they were younger. Their parents didn't work out because Nate's grandmother is a psycho. Anyway, they remained best friends even after their parents divorced."

She handed the vodka back to me. "I get the unrequited love thing. I'm not in love with him anymore, though. What fragile feelings I had left after years of hardly speaking to him, he decided to stomp on by saying hurtful things when he was drunk. They were true though. At least some of them were."

I couldn't imagine anything that could be said about her that would be negative. "He's a dick," I replied without even hearing what he'd said about her. Then I took a drink.

"Yes, he is."

We sat there a few minutes passing the vodka back and forth in silence. Thinking. Finally, I answered her question. "I think I realized I loved her when we were six. She had made a crown out of daisy's and put it on her head then danced around the yard. I watched her a long time wondering if anyone was as pretty as her. She finally saw me, stopped twirling, gave me a big smile and then held out her hand to me. She said she was the queen of the fairies and I could be her king. It's a silly memory, but it stuck with me."

I took a drink then. "Thanks for the vodka. It's helping." I passed it back to her.

"Yeah. We may not be able to walk back to the house, but you won't be hurting, and I won't be terrified of my adventure."

"Terrified? I thought you wanted this adventure."

She shrugged. "I wanted to be someone else. Do something completely unlike me. To get away. The reality of it scares me though."

"Then don't go."

A sad smile touched her face. "I have to. I need to."

"Because of him?" I asked.

"No," she shook her head. "Because of Lila. I need to do this for Lila. And I've had too much to drink on an empty stomach. I'm talking about myself in third person."

I laughed, and she joined me. It felt right sitting out here laughing being completely honest with each other.

Chapter Thirteen

♥ LILA KATE ♥

LIVE BAY WASN'T a long walk from Nate and Bliss's house. Which was a good thing because neither of us needed to be driving. The walk helped sober us up somewhat but not completely. It was a nice relaxed feeling. By the time we finished eating at the restaurant in front of Live Bay's bar, my head was much clearer. My concerns and fears were returning.

"I don't know if I'm up for dancing tonight," I told him.

"I don't think I'm up for the crowd there," he agreed.

At least he wasn't going to try and talk me into staying. But returning to Nate's where I would just sit and worry alone didn't seem appealing either.

"Let's get my truck and then go to my apartment. We can watch a movie. I have vodka. I also have some peanut butter ice cream in my freezer that needs to be eaten. It'll be quiet there."

That was better. "Okay. Yes, that sounds good. Especially the ice cream."

He smirked. "And I thought it would be my perfect personality that would win you over."

"That is just a plus. The ice cream definitely is the ultimate draw."

The server came, and Eli took the bill for our dinner and paid for it. This had been a date. A real one. Even after our drunken admissions on the beach. We talked about Sea Breeze and his childhood there on our way back to the truck. He had good memories of the place and a lot of friends who sounded a lot more colorful than the ones I had back home.

We didn't go inside or say anything to Bliss and Nate. Instead, we got in his truck and headed to his apartment which was more of a condo on the beach. Bliss had lived there with him before she got together with Nate. I wondered if he had bought a two bedroom just for that reason—for her.

But I didn't want to talk about that anymore, so I didn't ask.

"This is it. Movies are in that cabinet if you want to look through what I have. Or we can rent something from iTunes. Your choice."

It was a nice. You could tell a female had lived here once. There was a feminine touch that most guys didn't know how to pull off when they decorated. Or they didn't care to.

"I'll see what selection you have first," I told him walking over to the cabinet.

He left me in there. I opened the cabinet and saw the DVDs were in alphabetical order. He had a great selection. I found Top Gun toward the end and picked it up. I had seen this once when I was younger. It was a classic even back then.

Eli walked back into the room carrying a bottle of vodka, two glasses, and some cranberry juice. "I assume you don't always drink vodka straight out of the bottle," he said with a mischievous grin.

"You'd be correct. That was actually a first for me."

"Figured."

I handed him the DVD, and he nodded. "Nice choice," he

agreed then set the glasses on the coffee table and the vodka and cranberry juice behind them. "Help yourself. Want me to get the ice cream now? Or later?"

I wasn't hungry yet. I was still full from the fried crab claws and fries I had eaten. "I'm good with the vodka right now."

He sat down on the sofa then and waved his arm out beside him. "Then let's drink. I've sobered up, and I prefer the numbness that came with the vodka earlier."

"It definitely makes you brave. Which isn't necessarily a good thing," I said thinking about myself.

He handed me a glass with ice. "Fix it the way you like it. I have club soda too if you prefer that."

"Cranberry works just fine."

I poured what I thought was a shot of vodka then filled the rest of the glass with the juice. "We aren't very good influences on each other, are we?" I asked.

He chuckled. "Why? Because we keep drinking?"

I nodded.

"It's just the timing isn't that great for either of us."

I leaned back and crossed my legs to get comfortable before taking a drink. "No, I guess it's not."

He poured at least half a glass of the vodka and added just a splash of juice. Then he stood up and went over to the DVD player to put in the movie. Again, this was comfortable. It was easy to trust Eli.

The movie started, and we drank as we watched it. An hour into the movie, he stood up and went to get the ice cream. I still wasn't hungry, but I ate it. Another drink appeared in my hand and with it came the smooth, easy feeling. I enjoyed it and let him refill me again.

"Lila?"

"Yes?"

"What happened for real last night?"

I thought for a moment then figured there was no reason not to be honest with him. "We had sex on the beach. You used a condom."

He sat up straight and I let out a giggle. It was funny now. Or the vodka made me think it was.

"Was . . . was I any good?" he asked and that made me laugh harder. Of all the things for him to be worried about that wasn't what I thought it would be.

"Yes. You do fine under intoxication. But then I don't know what you're like sober."

His smile was dark and sexy. "We could find out."

I shook my head. "No, we can't."

He sighed and leaned back against the sofa. "Damn."

I fell asleep before the movie ended, but my night had been fun. The alcohol relaxed me, and I didn't dream, I just slept.

The sun was just beginning to rise when I opened my eyes. I was asleep on the sofa alone. A blanket was covering me and a pillow was under my head. I stretched, got up, folded the blanket and ran a hand through my hair. I needed to leave. Bliss and Nate were going to assume things that hadn't happened. Not that I should care. But a part of me did. And it had happened before, just not last night.

I found an old receipt and a pen in my purse.

Thanks for last night. It was fun. I hope it helped.

Lila

I placed the note on the table in front of me and then left. I liked Eli Hardy, and in different circumstances he'd be harder to leave. But his heart was taken even if he didn't want it to be.

My walk back to Nate and Bliss's was peaceful. The seagulls were out, and the smell of the salt in the air calmed me. The sun wasn't boiling yet, and I enjoyed just being alone. My thoughts were all over the place as I walked. So much so that I almost missed the motorcycle parked outside Nate's house.

When I did see it, I paused. I knew that bike. I also knew the guy straddling it. He turned his head and looked at me. Even though I hated it. Even though I would do anything for it not to affect me to see him there, my heart picked up just a little.

I took a deep breath then resumed walking toward the front door and Cruz Kerrington.

"What are you doing here?" I snapped when I was close enough for him to hear me.

He gave me his cocky grin. "I heard you were taking a road trip."

"So?"

"Why?"

I didn't want to answer him. But he was here. He had never come here. "Why are you here?" I demanded.

"Why did you take off?" Cruz countered.

I was the new Lila. I wasn't the same girl that I had left behind in Rosemary. "Because I don't want to be that girl anymore. The one you described."

"So you thought leaving town alone would change that?" He sounded amused.

I hated that. I hated his smug grin and self-confidence. "Yes. This is my . . . adventure. Now leave. Let me enjoy it."

Cruz didn't move. He studied me a moment. I started to walk past him toward the front door. "Get on, Lila," he said and I glanced back at him. He was holding out a helmet.

"Excuse me?" I asked thinking I'd heard him incorrectly.

"Get on the back of my bike," Cruz repeated.

"Are you crazy?"

He shrugged. "Yeah. But you know that already. Now get on the bike."

"I'm not getting on that bike."

He cocked one eyebrow at me. It was a sexy talent. "You said you wanted an adventure. What is more adventurous than climbing on my bike and just leaving?"

"Where would we go?" I heard myself ask.

"Anywhere, everywhere."

I shook my head again. "My bag is upstairs. My car is here."

"Yeah . . . but you want change. That's the old you. Climb on, and we'll find the new Lila Kate Carter."

I stood there. My head was telling me how ridiculous this was and that I needed to march inside and slam the door in his face, but my feet began moving toward him. I had nothing but the clothes I was wearing and the purse on my shoulder. I stopped beside his bike and he put the helmet on my head. Then his hand closed around mine. "Get on."

And I did.

Chapter Fourteen

~CRUZ KERRINGTON~

SOMETIMES YOU DO shit and you don't think it through. That's what got me here. I had just reacted. Now I had Lila Kate on my bike headed west to New Orleans. Once her daddy found out, I was damn sure I'd need to be put in protective custody. Grant Carter was going to kill me. But until then, I was going to be there while Lila Kate liberated her sweet little uptight ass.

At least she'd loosen up. I didn't want her to start dancing on bars topless or anything, but this was a step in the right direction. Just leaving all her shit. No explanation. Just driving out of there. I didn't think she'd do it. I hadn't been able to sleep. I'd gotten up at three and went outside with a backpack that held a change of clothes and a toothbrush then climbed on and drove off.

But dammit they'd just let her take off on her own. I didn't give one fuck that she was a grown woman. She was so sheltered that it didn't matter how old she was. I loved the fact she wanted to spread her wings some. She just needed a little guidance. That's why I was here. Grant should be thanking me. He wouldn't. He'd likely try to kill me.

We'd be in New Orleans by the time everyone woke up and realized she was gone. I'd have her call her momma, and I'd call Nate and tell him. I wasn't going to let everyone worry.

I pulled into a Wal-Mart parking lot and drove her up to the door before cutting the engine. "This is the best we'll find this early. Get some jeans and closed toed shoes. Change and come on back out."

She didn't move. "You want me to go in there and buy jeans and shoes?"

I turned around and pulled her helmet off. "You want to ride all the way to New Orleans dressed in those shorts and a pair of sandals?"

She looked down at her bare legs then lifted her eyes back to me. "I guess that's a bad idea?" It sounded like a question.

I nodded.

With a sigh, she got off the bike. "I should have at least got some of my things."

"Did you have jeans and boots packed?" I asked her, and she shook her head. "Didn't think so."

She walked inside, and I tried not to admire her ass. That was not what this was about. I'd been drunk when I kissed her. I wasn't going to play with her emotions. I cared too much about her to just make her one of the girls I'd fucked. Lila deserved romance. I didn't do romance.

I did ropes, and handcuffs, and strippers. That was my speed. Girls who knew I liked some rough play, and they wanted it too. Lila was breakable. Definitely, not my speed.

I thought about calling Nate now and decided not to. They were asleep. No need to let them all know I'd run off with Lila just yet. They'd know soon enough. She'd get her fucking adventure. Then she'd come back home safely.

Holy fuck.

I hadn't told her to find the tightest pair of jeans available and put them on. Lila Kate walked back to the bike. She was wearing black fake leather boots, but that didn't matter because the tight ass jeans she had on was all anyone could see. That and the equally tight tank top she was now wearing. It said "Speed" on the front and looked ripped at the neckline to show off her cleavage.

"What the hell?" I asked.

She grinned. "I think I look like a biker now."

She looked like she was going to get me in a damn fight. "Jesus," I muttered then handed her the helmet. She slid it on and then climbed on the back. "It's the best they had," she explained.

"What, they didn't have your size clothing?" I shot back.

"This is my size!"

"It looks a few sizes too small," I argued.

"It's supposed to be tight."

"Where are your other clothes?" I asked.

"I left them in the dressing room. Those where the old Lila Kate."

I didn't say any more. This adventure was what Lila Kate wanted to do. She was right, she was nothing like the old Lila. Nothing like her at all.

I pulled back onto the road and headed toward I-10. We needed to get some road behind us. Lila's arms were wrapped around me and her body wasn't pressed to my back exactly, but it was close. Close enough for me to feel it. Damn, I had to think about something else. This was about me getting the hell away from the club and all the responsibilities my dad wanted to throw at me. It was also about making sure Lila Kate came back alive.

The one thing I abso-fuckin-lutely knew it wasn't about was me touching Lila Kate. I felt my phone vibrate in my pocket and cursed. Someone had already woken up and realized I was gone.

More than likely it was my dad. He'd probably had another day of early morning golf torture planned for me.

He'd be pissed at first, but when I explained why I came to protect Lila Kate he was either going to understand or be even more pissed. That was a toss-up. I couldn't be sure yet. I didn't fucking care either. I was even gladder I'd woken up and left knowing if I'd stayed I would have had to play golf again today.

We entered Mississippi, and Lila Kate pointed at the sign as if that was exciting. I understood. She traveled via a plane most of the time. She hadn't been to places like Mississippi before. When we got to Biloxi, I headed toward Beauvoir—the Jefferson Davis Home and Presidential Library. It wasn't something I'd seen before or ever cared to see. But I knew Lila Kate liked history stuff. Museums and shit.

We pulled up in front of the large white house that had been restored to what it looked like in 1889 when he had lived in this house. I parked beside the only other car in the parking lot. It was a little after eight in the morning, and the sign said it opened at eight. No one was here yet.

Lila Kate pulled off her helmet and looked up at the place. "What are we doing?"

"You ever been to Biloxi?" I asked.

She shook her head.

"Then you should see a bit of it. Where the crazy ass confederates last president lived. There's a confederate cemetery here too."

She slowly moved her gaze from the house to me. "You brought me to see the home of Jefferson Davis?"

Maybe that had been a bad idea. Hell, I thought she liked history stuff. "Don't you like shit like this?"

She studied me a minute, and then she laughed. "Let's go look at the house," she finally said and put her helmet on her seat.

"What's so funny?" I asked her as I got off the bike. I was not going to look at her ass in those jeans. I wasn't. Dammit.

"That you brought me to a Confederate president's home."

"There weren't a lot of options. We are in the thick of the south here, Lila. This is the history they've got to see around here. Besides, it's impressive as hell. Look at it," I said as I gestured at the large building.

She turned back to the house and nodded. "Yes, it is. Let's see the place."

Chapter Fifteen

♥ LILA KATE ♥

AFTER SPENDING AN hour walking around the house and cemetery, Cruz then took me to eat breakfast at a casino. It was really good which surprised me. When we were walking back out to Cruz's bike, he glanced over at me. "So now you've seen some of Mississippi."

This behavior was so unlike the Cruz that I knew I had smiled big. Once Cruz had been nice. When we were kids I'd seen this side of him, but not since then. Seeing it again was . . . it was . . . dangerous. I had to remember who he was and keep my head straight.

The rest of the ride was fast. We entered Louisiana shortly after leaving Biloxi. At a red light, Cruz looked over his shoulder at me. "You want safe and fancy or do you want the atmosphere?"

"Atmosphere," I yelled through my helmet and over the engine.

"Good," he replied then took off toward a very scenic area that didn't smell that great, but it was exactly like I pictured. Considering I was recognizing things from The Originals that I was guilty of watching on a Netflix binge. I started to point something out but stopped myself. Cruz would have a blast making fun of me.

He pulled into a parking deck and cut the engine. I took off my helmet and looked around. "Where are we?"

"Hotel parking."

I didn't see a hotel. "Are you sure?"

"Yeah, I'm sure. Been here before. A couple of times."

"Why were you in New Orleans?" I asked.

He smirked at me. "Mardi Gras."

Ah. I should have guessed. "This won't be nearly as exciting as I had imagined."

He got of the bike. "There won't be women showing me their tits all over the street. So yeah, it'll be less exciting."

I rolled my eyes and got off the bike. "I have nothing with me. I need to find a store to buy some toiletries, and a change of clothes would be nice."

"Let's get a room, then we can go shopping."

"Rooms," I corrected him.

He cocked an eyebrow. "Seriously? We're gonna waste money on two rooms?"

I nodded. "Yes, we seriously are."

"Jesus, Lila Kate. I'm not going to try and screw you. I've never tried and I'm not about to start now."

That stung. I wasn't going to let him know it stung, but it did. "I'm aware you're not attracted to me. You've made that very clear. I like my privacy. I don't want to share a room with you."

He shrugged. "Whatever."

There was the guy I knew. At least he was reminding me that the sweet guy who had wanted me to experience some of Mississippi was a brief lapse. The Cruz I knew and disliked was back.

We checked in without saying much to each other. Our rooms were beside each other. When we got to the doors to our rooms, he looked over at me. "This gonna be too close for you? Planning on sneaking in some guy off the street you find and don't want me to see?"

He was being a smartass. This Cruz I knew well. But the new Lila Kate wasn't going to take his smart mouth. I unlocked the door and just before walking inside my room met his cocky gaze. "No. This is fine. My last one night stand was on a public beach. I figure if I can have sex on a public beach then I can have sex in the room next to yours." I didn't give him a chance to respond. I quickly went inside my room and closed the door behind me.

I almost expected him to knock on my door to ask me what I was talking about. He didn't. But I knew he was thinking about it. I had nothing to unpack. But I did use a towel and some facial soap to wash my face. Then I got in the shower and bathed the road scum off me. I washed my panties in the shower then hung them up to dry.

I'd have to go without until we went to a store. Walking over to the window with the bath towel wrapped around me, I took my phone and snapped a photo of the French Quarter. Then I texted it to Eli.

Arrived. It's just like I pictured it. Sorry I didn't say goodbye.

I needed to call Nate and Bliss to explain. Then, of course, my parents.

I started to dial Nate's number when Eli texted me back.

You left already? was his response.

I sighed. He hadn't even gone looking for me when he woke up and I was gone. I don't know why I expected him to. He had other things on his mind.

I didn't respond to him. I called Nate instead.

"Just got off the phone with Cruz," was Nate's greeting. "Your dad is going to kill him. You thought of that?"

I sighed. I had considered that. But at the moment, I wasn't thinking about anything other than doing something completely out of character. Something exciting and I did it. But there was going to be hell to pay later.

"I'll handle my dad. I'm sorry I didn't leave a note or get my things."

"Cruz thinks he's protecting you. That's all this is Lila."

Nate knew. I'd never told him, but he knew. He had been part of our trio as kids. He saw it even though Cruz never saw the little girl crush in my eyes. Nate was always more observant. Now he was making sure grown Lila Kate didn't get the wrong notion that she had a chance with Cruz.

"I know." I didn't say more. It was embarrassing.

"I got your Rover in my garage, and your things will be in the guest bedroom until you return."

"Thanks, Nate. Tell Bliss I'm sorry for running off without a goodbye."

"I will. She gets it. Better than me I think."

We said our goodbyes and ended the call. I wasn't in the mood to talk to my parents yet. I was an adult. The money I was using was mine. I didn't have to call them. I was free to be my own woman.

I felt guilty but I dropped my phone back on the bed and went to put my clothes back on without the panties. That wasn't going to feel very good in jeans. I had to find a store.

Chapter Sixteen

~CRUZ KERRINGTON~

I REALIZED THE jeans hadn't been bad as Lila Kate came walking out of the department store wearing a short black skirt with a sleeveless silver top that tied above her navel. Then the heels. Did she really plan on walking around New Orleans in those heels?

I was still trying to decide if her "sex on the beach" comment had been completely made up or she'd been as serious as she looked when she said it. That was completely irresponsible. If she had then she was even more naïve than I ever thought.

"That's completely functional," I drawled trying not to be annoyed that most of her body was on display. I could see men turning their heads to check her out without even looking at them. I knew men. I was one. And I wanted to look at her too.

She lifted one bare shoulder as if I knew nothing. "I thought so."

She had two other bags in her hands. I was carrying the one full of her toiletries she'd picked up at a pharmacy before we walked to this place. "Don't get any more shit. That's all that is going to fit on my bike."

"This is plenty," she told me. "Let's drop it off at the hotel then I want to see Bourbon Street. "

Of course, she did.

We headed back from where we came and she seemed completely fine with the idea of walking in those damn heels. Didn't they hurt? I decided to let it go and asked something else I'd been putting off. "You talked to your parents?"

I was expecting her to say "yes," she called them as soon as she got to the room. Instead, she shook her head no.

"They're probably worried," I pointed out.

She shrugged. "I'm grown."

That was not a Lila Kate response. I couldn't decide if I liked this change or not. I'd grown up knowing there were two things I could depend on. That my dad was never going to make me forget what was expected of me. And that Lila Kate Carter was going to always do the right thing.

She'd just blown that out of the water.

"You've been grown awhile. What made you decide to embrace it?"

She didn't look at me. She kept her gaze straight ahead. "Life."

That was all she was going to say. Life. As if that made sense. I was in New Orleans babysitting her, and she was dressing like . . . like . . . like a fucking girl I'd pick up in a club, giving me one-word answers, and rebelling against everything she'd ever done.

I pushed for more answers. "What inspired this fit of rebellion?"

The pinched frown that came over her face was interesting. There was something, but I doubted if she was going to tell me. At least not yet. Our journey had just begun. Eventually, she'd tell me.

"I'd rather not talk about it," was her final answer.

I didn't push. I would let it go for now. "Fine. So tell me what is it you want to see on Bourbon Street?"

This brought a smile to her face. "I have no idea. I just want to see it. And can we get beignets? I've always wanted to try the real things."

"Yeah, we can. Beignets are better if you eat them sober. Let's do that before we hit Bourbon Street."

I expected her to tell me she didn't plan on drinking. But she didn't. She just nodded in agreement. Jesus. I hoped she wasn't planning on getting drunk. Not dressed like that.

"How far can you walk in those shoes?" I asked.

"Miles."

I started to argue and decided to let it go. If she wanted to walk in them, it wasn't my business. Her toes could hate her later.

Lila Kate dropped her bags off quickly. She grinned like a little kid on our way to get beignets. I kept waiting for her to complain about the shoes she was wearing, but she never did. She seemed completely taken in with the scenery around her. Watching her experience New Orleans was more fun than my first trip. She was soaking it in. We had to stop to watch a group of guys doing a street show, flipping over people. Then we had to stop to watch a kid dance. Both times she left tips and clapped excitedly. It was fucking cute. That was the side of Lila Kate I knew. The innocence that only she made appear beautiful.

When the white powder from the beignets got all over her hands and shirt, she laughed as if it was the best thing that had happened all day. She dusted it off with ease, and then asked if there were places to go dancing.

Night had finally started to fall, and it was time to take her to the center of it all. Lila's wide-eyed wonder as we entered Bourbon Street from Canal Street made me wish I had a fucking camera. Just to remember this. I needed a drink. My head was getting all fucked up. I needed to drink and get shit straight. Not think about taking photos of Lila.

"We'll start here and make our way down," I told her turning into a bar with live music. It was hit or miss with these places. You just had to go in them all until you found the best music. Most of them had the same drinks.

Lila beamed as we walked into the first bar. It was already crowded; the music playing was old eighties rock. I went directly to the bar. "What do you want?" I asked her.

"I don't know. What do you suggest?"

"You've drunk before, Lila.

"Yes, but I always order the same thing. I want to do something different. Be someone different."

"We're in New Orleans. Why don't you try a hurricane?"

"Sounds good to me."

I wasn't into drinking the sweet shit, but most girls liked that kind of drink. I ordered a Jack Daniels and a hurricane. The bartender was a female with creamy tan skin and clear blue eyes. The top she was wearing left little to the imagination, and I didn't mind enjoying the view. When she turned to get my order, she winked at me and although I knew those lashes were fake they were hot. So were her ass cheeks hanging out of the shorts she had on. God, I loved Bourbon Street.

I glanced back to see Lila Kate studying the place as if she needed to memorize every detail. She was fine, so I turned my attention back to the bartender. She swung her hips as she walked back my way carrying the drinks. "I get off at two," she said as she slid them in front of me.

"I'll remember that," I replied and gave her a fifty. "I don't need change."

She looked over my shoulder. "The girl with you?"

"A friend," I replied.

"Well, your friend may need some help," the bartender told me. Snapping my attention off her nipples I could see through the thin fabric of her shirt, I looked around to find Lila Kate.

Two guys were saddled up beside her doing their pretty boy flirting. She seemed nervous but was smiling and talking to them. When her eyes swung over in my direction, I saw the uncertainty there, and I moved toward her.

This was going to be a long night. Maybe I should have ordered a double.

Chapter Seventeen

♥ LILA KATE ♥

"IT'S THE FUCKING clothes," Cruz muttered to me after he handed me my drink then slipped his arm around my waist and moved me away from the two guys who had been trying to convince me to come to some frat party they were having nearby.

"What is?" I asked confused.

"The guys. You dress like that, and you're gonna have guys swarming."

He sounded annoyed. After I had just watched him all but drool over the bartender who might as well have been wearing a bikini. Or heck, topless. I could see through her thin white shirt from where I was and she wasn't wearing a bra. I looked classy compared to her.

"There is nothing wrong with my clothes," I spat back at Cruz. Then took another drink of the delicious concoction he'd gotten me.

"Skirts too short and you're showing off your stomach."

I spun around and glared at him. "That waitress you were

ogling is barely clothed. Her bottom is hanging out of her shorts! And you're saying I'm not dressed okay? But you enjoyed seeing her naked boobs through that top that is pointless."

He scowled. "You're not like her."

What the heck? "You are a pig!" I yelled then stormed past him into the street. I needed my distance because I was tempted to toss this red drink in his face.

"Lila!" he called out behind me. I kept stalking off. I had no idea where I was going, but I was going somewhere. "Lila, for Christ sake stop!"

I ignored him.

"You're being dramatic," he said and I thought about that. Maybe I was a touch sensitive. So I slowed down. This street was packed with people, and as exciting as it seemed it probably wasn't safe for me to get lost on.

"All I am saying is you look . . ." he paused and rubbed his temples with his thumb and forefinger. "You look like fucking Snow White has decided to go naughty. Okay? It's very fucking erotic to see someone who looks like you dressed in something like that. The waitress in there—a guy expects her to dress that way. She looks like a porn star. You look like a Disney Princess dressed up like a porn star, and that is exciting to a man. Don't ask me why. I can't explain it. We are all bastards, okay?"

I studied him letting his words sink in. Then I started to laugh. I couldn't help myself. It wasn't the drink because I'd barely drank any of it. The way he had just described me was hilarious.

"Why are you laughing?" he asked, his face frustrated and confused.

I caught my breath and then laughed some more. He watched me like I had lost my mind. When I could finally breathe enough to form a sentence, I said, "You just called me a Disney Princess porn star."

Cruz kept his frown at first, and then he slowly started to grin. "It was the best example I had."

I took a sip of my drink. "I don't look like Snow White."

"Yeah, Lila, you do. I once wondered if birds dressed you every morning. I was eight at the time, so it made sense back then."

I laughed again. I had to. He was right. The old Lila was very Snow White-like. She was proper, poised, polite. And boring. That was my past though.

"Okay, I agree. I was very Snow White-like but not anymore."

Cruz stopped smiling. "Yeah, I noticed."

"Let's try this again," I suggested. Then pointed at a bar across the street. "Let's try there," I suggested.

"No way in hell," he said as he took my elbow. "I'll pick the place."

"What was wrong with that place?"

"I'm not ready to take you into a topless bar."

Oh. "Okay, yeah. You better pick the place." I agreed.

"How's your drink?"

"Good. Sweet," I told him.

"Yeah. Never tried a hurricane. I don't like sweet," Cruz said then steered me into another bar with open doors and live music. This time it was more Cajun type music. "I need another drink. You're coming with me."

I followed along beside him, and this time the bartender was a man. However, he also was checking Cruz out. I didn't blame him. Cruz was something to look at. I just didn't let myself look at him. At least not for long.

I scanned the place, watching the people dancing and drank more of my hurricane.

"Come on, Snow White," he said once he had his drink.

We walked over and found a tall table with two empty stools and sat down. The beat was different than anything I had danced to so I watched the people who knew how to dance to that music. I learned quickly. Once I was sure I could do it, I finished my drink.

"I'm going to dance," I told him as I stood up.

"To that? You can't dance like that," Cruz argued.

I wasn't secure about a lot of things, but I was confident in my ability to dance. Feeling the buzz from my drink, I winked at him then walked out to the dance floor where others were dancing. The song started up and I joined in. The style of dance was easy to pick up, and before long I had forgotten about Cruz, Eli and everything else. I was just having fun. Letting go. Being someone else. Someone who didn't live the same old everyday life.

"You from around here?" a guy asked me after a song ended. He was tall with long dreadlocks and big brown eyes. His thick accent told me he was from around here.

"No," I replied.

"Who taught you to dance like that?" he asked looking impressed.

"I'm a dancer. I watched and learned."

"You shouldn't be dancing alone."

I started to say more when the music started back up. He held out his hand and raised his eyebrows as if he was issuing an invitation. I raised mine, and placed my hand in his. I didn't feel like me at all. I loved it.

We began dancing together, and before I realized it, everyone else had moved back and given us the center of the floor. I was twirled and dipped, and we moved like we'd done this dance together before. I had no idea what it was called, but I let him lead and I followed. I heard whistles and clapping. It just kept me going. Once the song ended, my dance partner tilted me back and placed a kiss directly on my lips. That startled me.

I stood up quickly and forced a smile, then turned to walk away, but ran right into Cruz's arms. He was glaring at my dance partner over my shoulder. "You're either gonna get me killed or arrested," he muttered under his breath for only me to hear him. Then he slid his arm around my waist and we left the bar. Back outside and onto the street.

Chapter Eighteen

~CRUZ KERRINGTON~

BOURBON STREET HAD always been fun for me. Tonight was more stressful than fun. Why was I so damn overprotective of Lila? I had barely drunk anything. I stopped at the next bar and ordered a double shot of whiskey. I needed to lighten up. Enjoy this. If she wanted to dance with strangers, she could, and I would let her. I hadn't come to be a fucking babysitter. I wanted to have some fun too.

"I want something too. No sugar though. Maybe a Goose with soda," she said over the noise.

I had caught myself before I asked her if she'd had too much. I was acting like the damn hall monitor again. Instead, I ordered it and handed it to her. Then I walked over to the woman that had shots stuck in her naked cleavage and handed her a twenty-dollar bill. She waved her hand for me to assume the position on the table in front of her, then she climbed on top of me straddling my waist and stuck the shot of whiskey in her tits before leaning down to pour it in my mouth.

The people around us cheered. After I slugged back that shot

I handed her another twenty from my pocket and we did it one more time. The buzz from her large tan breasts in my face mixed with the whiskey had me feeling like myself. I winked at her, and she brushed her almost bare nipple over my mouth while smiling at me wickedly before climbing off me.

When I stood up, I had to take a moment to steady myself. "You come on back when you want some more," she said her accent thick and exotic.

"You keep talking to me, and I might never leave," I told her.

She lifted both breasts and shook them at me. Damn, I loved this place. I picked up my drink that was on the table and finished it off. I remembered Lila Kate, but the concern for her safety had eased off a bit. I scanned the area expecting to see her off dancing again with some stranger, but I didn't see her at all. I was feeling relaxed and more than a little turned on. Not being able to spot her snatched that feeling away real damn fast.

I looked through the crowd again, but she was nowhere.

"Your girl left. Don't think she was a fan of watching you drink from another woman's boobs." I jerked my head to the left to see a tall redhead with a disgusted look on her face. "Can't say I blame her," the woman said as she pointed at the exit to her right. "She went out there before the second shot."

I should have thanked her or corrected her assumption, but I did neither. I hurried for the door Lila had left out of hoping she hadn't gone far. This street was getting packed already and finding her among all these people and all these bars would be difficult if not impossible.

I just wanted to have some fun, and she couldn't let me have it. She couldn't stay fucking put for a few minutes. Jesus, she was more trouble than I'd anticipated. Her dark hair was the first thing I saw when I stepped out of the bar. She was standing by a street light only a few feet from the bar.

Her arms were crossed over her chest, and her shoulders slightly bent. Like she was cold and trying to keep warm. That couldn't be it though because it was hot as fuck out here.

"Lila!" I called to her. She slowly turned to look at me and then resumed her stance—like she saw me but wasn't interested in me at all. Or like she was pissed.

I took the few steps to reach her, ready to ask what the hell she had been thinking coming out here alone. But when I got to her she dropped her arms and kept her gaze on everything and anything but me. "Ready for the next bar?" she asked.

She was upset. It was in her tone. "Why did you just walk out?" I asked frustrated by this whole scenario. I'd just started enjoying myself.

"I didn't like that bar."

What? "You don't like a place so you just leave. You couldn't wait to tell me?"

"You were busy." The sarcasm dripping from her voice wasn't missed.

"I was just starting to enjoy myself. Jesus, Lila."

She started walking away then. Like she was angry and wanted to get away from me. I'd done nothing wrong. "Then go back in there and have fun. If that's what you want to do, I have no problem with it." The tone or her voice didn't sound like she had no problem with it.

I reached out and grabbed her arm, stopping her. "What is with you? Are you pissed that I drank shots from that girl's tits? That's what she's there for. Some of the bars here have a lot more than that. It was tame. I wasn't hurting anyone."

She sighed heavily, and then finally turned to look at me. "That's what you like?"

"Drinking shots from a woman's cleavage? Yes, so do all heterosexual men on the fucking planet."

"You don't know her."

"No, but that doesn't really matter."

She studied me a moment. "Have you ever been in love, Cruz?"

What the fuck? How had we gone from me liking whiskey between tits to love? "No, but what the hell's that got to do with this conversation?"

The way she was studying me made me uncomfortable. Like she could see more than I wanted. "Because it seems shallow."

"It's sexy, fun. It's not supposed to be anything more."

Lila didn't reply to that. I let her pull her arm out of my grasp. She finally nodded. "Okay." I wasn't sure what she meant by "okay" and if that was her way of ending this ridiculous talk we were having then good.

"Let's go find more sexy and fun things to do," she said as she began walking again.

I fell into step beside her. She went to the very next bar and didn't wait for me to order a drink. Instead, she went straight to the bar and ordered a double shot of whiskey for herself, downed it in one very long gulp, then ordered another.

"Unless you want me holding back your hair out there on the street you need to slow down," I warned. She ignored me and drank the next one exactly the same way. After that, she left me ordering my own drink and walked out to the dance floor. I placed my order with the bartender then watched in shock as Lila Kate let a man take her hand and put her up on a table. The guy on stage called out "What you want to hear sweet thing?"

She gave him a big saucy smile I'd never seen on Lila Kate before. "Poison," she yelled out.

Poison? What the fuck was she doing?

"I think I'm in love!" the guy on stage shouted Then the band started up, and so did Lila. I knew all about her dancing. She'd done it her whole life. It was what paid for her college. But what I didn't know was that beyond the ballet and other fancy shit she'd learned that somewhere along the way, Lila Kate had learned to do something that would make her millions if she ever decided to take her clothes off and take up a career dancing on a pole. Motherfucker.

After I pulled my jaw off the floor, I had to fight the urge to take her off that table and away from all the catcalls and whistling and cheering. Was it sexy as hell? Yes. More so than anything I'd ever seen. Back to the Snow White gone bad thing I'd tried to explain to her earlier. But it wasn't Lila. She had class. She wasn't the kind of girl who did things like this.

I held out until some drunk bastard reached up and ran his hand up her calf. Then I was done. She'd made whatever goddamn point she had wanted to make and I didn't need to see anymore. I stalked through the crowd, and after shoving two guys back, I grabbed her legs and threw her over my shoulder.

She squealed.

"Hey! Put the woman down!" A guy who had been admiring the view said standing in my path.

"She's with me. We are traveling together. She's mine," I replied giving him a warning glare.

"Are you okay with him taking you?" the guy on the stage asked.

"Yes," she said sounding annoyed.

"Let her go, guys," the lead singer said, and my path was cleared. "If she was mine I'd have taken her too."

Chapter Nineteen
♥ LILA KATE ♥

JUST BECAUSE I let him haul me out of there like a caveman didn't mean I wasn't angry. I was furious. He could have a good time but I couldn't. There were rules I was missing. He liked girls to show off their body and flaunt it, but I wasn't allowed to flaunt mine.

When we were far enough away from the bar that he wasn't going to get in a fight, I slapped his back and started wiggling to be set free. "Let me down!"

He stopped walking and put me on my feet. "Can I trust you're not going to jump on a pole somewhere and take off your clothing?" he snapped at me.

That was it. I hadn't asked him to come to Sea Breeze. I had left because of something he had said. He was the reason I ran in the first place. He had accused me of being cold and icy. And when I did what it was he obviously liked from women, he got angry. I couldn't win. Not with him.

"What? Was that too clean for you? Would you rather I go in there and jerk my top off and start giving out shots in my cleavage?"

His expression was one you gave someone who was mentally unstable. "Fuck no!"

"Then what is it that you like Cruz? You call me icy and say I'm untouchable. Breakable. I take off to prove I'm none of those things. Then when I get brave and loosen up and do things like that in there, you act as if I'm doing something wrong. I don't get it. I wish I didn't care. I have tried not to care for so long I can't even remember when I didn't. You. It's always been you. I hate that. I hate that it's you. Why couldn't it be someone else? Someone who was like . . . like . . . Eli! Someone like him. Why can't I want someone like Eli? What is so wrong with my head that I have always wanted you?" The words were coming out. I heard myself, and I knew I should shut up. That what I was saying could never be taken back. But it was like I'd handed control of my mouth over to someone else, and they were failing at their job. Because even when I tried to stop, it got worse.

"Is it how I look? Am I not pretty enough? Do you prefer another type? Maybe it's my breasts—maybe because they aren't as large as the girl in the bar? Is that it? What about me makes you treat me like a school marm? Please tell me so I can fix it!"

People were ignoring us. They walked right past us, and when I was done ranting, I realized I had just yelled all of that for anyone around us to hear. Someone called out, "I think you're fucking sexy, baby. Come on over here."

I tuned that out. This street was full of drunks. I was one of them apparently because I had just said stuff I'd never ever say sober. I had too much pride. Drunken Lila Kate had no pride. I wish I'd realized that sooner.

"You're not cheap. You're not easy. You're like a rare fucking diamond. You want me? You want my attention? Why? I'm a mess. I can't be what you deserve. I don't even know how. And if I let myself touch you, enjoy what you just did in there, I'll be ruined. You think you want me, but if you really knew me you'd change your mind. Then I would have had a taste of you and nothing would ever compare to that again. You terrify me. Scare me like nothing has ever scared me in my life." His eyes were bright and wild. His hand was trembling as I dropped my gaze to stare at it, unable to keep our gazes locked. Everything else on him seemed tight. Stiff.

"I do know you. I've watched you my entire life. I've seen you at your worst and your best." I didn't yell those words. I just said them and let them hang there while I continued to let his words soak in. I hadn't expected that from him. I still wasn't sure if I might be dreaming. Could I be passed out drunk somewhere?

"I don't do relationships, Lila."

I lifted my gaze then. "I'm not asking for one."

He seemed torn. His eyes narrowed. "Then what is it you want from me?"

I wanted many things. And I knew he'd never give me what I wanted. We would never have a happily ever after. That wasn't Cruz. It never had been. "Now. Just now. This trip. Nothing more."

He didn't respond right away. He stood there staring at me like he didn't believe me. He shouldn't because I wanted more. I just knew I'd never get that. I wasn't the girl to make him want more. He'd meet her one day and he'd change his mind. He'd be able to be that guy. The one who did relationships.

I'd heard my parents story a million times. My dad hadn't been that guy either. My mom had been the one to change his mind. It happened to all of them eventually. I knew I wasn't that one for Cruz and I should let it go and walk away. But I couldn't. I wanted to know for just a moment. How it felt to be with him. There was a chance I'd get him out of my head and heart then. I'd move on and find someone else. That Cruz Kerrington wouldn't always be in my thoughts.

"Nothing but this trip?" he repeated my words like a question. I nodded.

"Did you hear the part about ruining me?"

I gave a small shrug. "We both know that won't happen. I'm not the one. You haven't found her yet."

He frowned. "The one?"

"Yes. The one. The girl you'll want forever with."

He shook his head. "You're messing with my head. I swear."

"Are you attracted to me?" I asked him boldly. I could thank those double shots of whiskey for that.

"That's not the point here. I don't know if I can . . . can just have a fling with you, Lila. There are feelings there. I don't like fucking feelings. Not with women. I can't hurt you, and that's what I'll do."

I took a step toward him, placed a hand on his chest. This was a gamble, but I was brave right now. I wouldn't be in the morning. I'd gone this far I needed to push further. "You can't hurt me if I know the rules. We enjoy this. Have a fling. Then move on like we've always been."

He dropped his gaze to my hand. "What if you ruin me?"

"Take a chance," I whispered.

"Fuck," he muttered in reply. Then his hand wrapped around my wrist, and he jerked me up against his body. I barely had time to catch my breath before his mouth was on mine. The taste of our drinks mixed with the headiness that I had won. For now, I had this. It was my decision, and I hoped that this got him out of my system so that I could eventually move on.

"No more bars," he said against my mouth. "Back to the hotel. And we're not staying in two fucking rooms."

I didn't argue. I just gave a nod of my head in agreement. This was it. It better not be a dream.

Chapter Twenty

~CRUZ KERRINGTON~

THERE WERE SMART decisions and stupid decisions. And then there were mistakes. I wasn't sure where this one landed, but with Lila in my arms smelling like heaven, and the image of her dancing on that table was all that I cared about, at the moment.

I broke the kiss, grabbed her elbow and headed for the hotel. We were staying at a hotel just a few blocks ahead on the corner of Canal and Bourbon. I realized, as I all but ran without speaking, that deep down I was worried she'd sober up and change her mind. If I were half the fucking man I should be, I wouldn't let her do this tonight while she was drunk . . . while I was drunk.

But I'd tried to tell her what a screw up I was. She seemed to see more in me than was there. I wanted there to be more. I wanted to meet her expectations. When I was a kid, I had seen the look in her eyes, and I knew she saw me differently than she saw Nate. I loved that. I was different. It made me feel important. Then I'd kissed her, and it had scared me.

I knew then Lila Kate wasn't for me. I wasn't the kind of guy she'd want for long. She'd see too much eventually. It would change her mind. And she'd never gaze at me with that dreamy look in her eyes again. The idea I could lose that caused me to put a wall there. One built by hurting her. It had worked. Until now. Until I'd heard she'd left town and I chased after her, because I couldn't stand the idea of her finding a life without me in it.

As we entered the hotel, I paused and glanced down at her. The girl from my childhood. The girl I'd always watched but never allowed myself to get close to. The one I pretended like I didn't know why she avoided me.

"Are you sure?" I asked her.

"Yes."

I waited. I needed her to think. Let it all sink in. "We could sleep tonight. Wait until the morning."

She smiled. A soft one that made her eyes glow and made me feel like more of a man than I should. "Tonight," she finally said.

Fuck if I could ignore that. We would have tonight. If she regretted it in the morning, it might break me. But I was willing to chance it.

The trip up to her room was short but so many thoughts ran through my mind it felt much longer than it was. She touched her card key to the lock and it flashed green. This was it.

The door opened. We walked inside. My room was identical to this one. Just next door. I'd made a joke about it when we checked in. I wasn't joking now. I should be in that room. Alone. It was the right thing to do.

"Lila," I said thinking I should stop this.

She dropped her small shoulder purse on the floor then took the bottom of her shirt and pulled it up over her head. The white lace bra was small and the swell of her breasts looked as if they were about to spill out over the top exposing her nipples. Her shirt dropped to the floor beside her then she reached around and unsnapped her bra. I watched with fascination as the straps slid down her thin tan arms until her bra joined her shirt on the floor. Her round dark nipples pebbled from the chill of the room or from her excitement drawing my attention.

I moved, closing the space between us. Unable to keep my hands to myself I covered both her breasts with my hands. Although my hands were large they weren't large enough to take each breast completely. The excess excited me and I squeezed letting the softness tease my hands.

"Fuck me," her voice caught as she said the words. Those weren't words I ever imagined coming from her lips. They didn't fit Lila Kate. But the way her voice shook as she said them. The way she leaned into me and a soft moan escaped her simply from my touch made this all seem right. Like it was supposed to be. Like we were supposed to be.

The restraint I had held onto snapped. The naughty side of Lila was too much for a man to take. I grabbed her skirt and jerked it down until she stood there in nothing but a pair of black lace panties. They did little to cover her. Almost pointless unless trying to seduce a man. And I was seduced. I jerked my own shirt off and tossed it away.

My hands wrapped around her waist and I picked her up and carried her over to the office desk because it was closer than the bed. I sat her down, then pulled her panties off memorizing the way they looked as they slid off her body.

She shivered and my dick throbbed. This was Lila Kate . . . sweet, innocent, precious Lila Kate. Naughty, wild, needy Lila Kate had taken her place tonight, and I was trembling with anticipation. "What do you want?" I asked her as I unsnapped my jeans. "Tell me exactly what you want me to do."

Her eyes went from my bare chest and then locked on my pants as I began to loosen them, then I shoved them down my hips and stepped out of them. "Tell me, Lila," I demanded. I wasn't sure why I needed her to say, it but I did. I wanted her to talk dirty. Hear that pretty mouth say bad things. I was very likely to explode at the sound, but I wanted it.

"I want you," she whispered.

"You'll have to do better than that. Tell me."

She swallowed hard and lifted her gaze from my erection pressing through my boxer briefs to my eyes. "I told you. I want you to fuck me, Cruz."

That should be enough. I should be happy. But she'd turned me into a sex crazed monster. "You want it gentle?" I asked shoving my briefs down letting my thickened cock free.

She shook her head slowly. Her eyes wide as she stared at me. "No," her voice was so soft I almost didn't hear her.

"Tell me," I said as I pushed her thighs apart with my hands and stepped between them. "How do you want to be fucked?" At that last word, her eyes blazed with the same desire I felt.

"Hard. Fuck me hard."

My hands reached under her and grabbed her ass as I slammed into her. That one thrust was like sinking into warm tight satin. "Fuck!" I yelled as her body reacted to the sudden entry by squeezing my dick. It was better than my imagination.

Her small hands grabbed my arms, nails digging into my flesh. The sting felt amazing. "AH!" she cried out.

"Is that how hard you want it?" I growled near her ear wanting to pound into her over and over again but doing all I could to control myself.

"Yes. More," she panted.

My fingers dug into the flesh of her ass as I pulled back and plunged deeper. Groaning in pleasure, I bit her shoulder, and she began to beg. "Please, harder. I want to feel you there tomorrow."

Any sanity I was holding onto left. I picked her up sinking

her deeper onto my rigid cock and carried her to the bed where I dropped to the softness with her. Not wanting to pull away. I had to pull out in one quick movement and flip her on her stomach. "Ass in the air," I ordered.

She did it without question. On all fours, she stuck it up higher and I was hammering inside her immediately. Her cries became more frantic as did my breathing. I slapped her ass as hard as I could without really meaning to hurt her. Just to make it sting.

"Oh God!" she screamed. "I'm coming!" her body began to shake and her climax pulsed with my dick still locked inside her. I shook with the need to explode. It felt so fucking amazing it was all I could think about. Just before I lost the small amount of control I had left, I pulled back until I was free from her and cried out her name as my load covered her upturned ass.

Her body was still quivering, and my legs were weak. Too weak to move. We stayed there. Her head now rested on the bed. All that could be heard was both of us gasping for breath. That had been more. Much more than I expected. It had been addicting. I could tell myself it was too dangerous to do this again, but I'd be a fool. I wanted more. Hell, I wanted more as soon as I could take a deep breath again.

She began to lower her entire body to the bed.

"I need to clean you," I told her enjoying the look of my seed on her skin.

"M'kay," she said softly, still sinking until she was pressed completely against the mattress.

Smiling at the simple beauty of it I found the strength to stand and went to the bathroom to get a wet washcloth. I cleaned her quickly then covered her up. She lifted her head and looked at me. "You're coming to bed too?"

Lila's always perfect hair was mused. Her eyes were heavy, the lashes fanned her cheeks. The flush on her face was still there, and nothing had ever looked so damn beautiful in my life. "Yeah. I am."

I climbed in beside her and covered us both pulling her back against my chest. I'd be hard in a few fucking minutes, but she'd be asleep too soon to notice. I inhaled the smell of her hair and her hand covered mine.

It took less than two minutes for her breathing to slow. She was asleep in my arms, and I knew nothing would ever be the same for me. The ruin I had feared was much worse than that. I wasn't ever going to be able to let go.

Chapter Twenty-One

♥ LILA KATE ♥

HIS SMELL I recognized before I even opened my eyes. The warmth from his arms made me sigh and sink in closer. This had been better than I dreamed. And I had dreamed about this more than I cared to admit. Reminding myself it was for a short time, that it wasn't forever caused a sharp pain of loss so I pushed it away. For now, I would enjoy this time I did have. Each moment we had together, I would soak it all in.

"If you keep squirming closer we're gonna fuck before we get fully awake," his sleepy voice startled me, and I giggled. I never giggled, but I did then. It felt nice. Last night the alcohol had given me the courage I needed. This morning there were no regrets. No wishing it had been different. Because after opening up to him and walking back to the hotel I had sobered enough. I remembered every detail. I'd never forget a moment.

"Lila," his deep raspy voice warned as I pressed my body further into him. "You've got to be sore," he said as he kissed my shoulder.

I was. "It's a good sore."

He inhaled sharply then rolled on top of me. His naked body loomed over me. His hair messy and his eyes still heavy from sleep. "You've found your naughty mouth and you like it, don't you?" he asked as his knee opened my thighs.

I nodded.

Then he was inside me. That fast. I closed my eyes tightly, and gasped from the tenderness and the pleasure.

"Hurt?" he asked as he stayed completely still.

"Yes. But like I said, a good pain," I told him opening my eyes back to look at him. "Make it hurt more."

"Jesus, Lila. You're gonna kill us both," he groaned as he began to move. Pumping his hips in and out of me. His mouth trailed kisses over my collarbone and up my neck. His warm breath on my ear only heightened the feeling. "Say more dirty shit from that pretty mouth," he said in a whisper before nibbling on my ear.

I opened my legs wider lifting my knees to lock on his hips. "I want to feel you come inside me. To feel the heat from your release spill down my thighs," I told him, and he froze.

"Fuck, Lila. Don't say that kind of shit if you don't want me to explode."

"I do want you to explode."

His arms shook as he held himself completely still. "Are you on birth control?"

I smiled up at him. "Yes. I don't want to be a mommy any time soon."

He moved then, his expression fierce. "I'm clean. I'd never have touched you without a condom if I didn't know I was completely clean."

I trusted him. He was a lot of things, but he wouldn't put me in any danger. I knew that. "Then come inside me."

His hips began to pound against me. All other thoughts fell away. All I felt was the climb to my own climax. I could hear his breath deepen and his muttered curse words. I opened my eyes and atched his arms flex with each movement.

When I jerked up against him and wrapped my legs around his waist to hold him there, I cried out his name.

"Goddamn, Lila," he swore, and then I felt it. All of it as he gave me exactly what I had begged for. I wanted this to last forever. I wouldn't think about the day it would all end. Because at this moment, I had it all.

He rolled to the side taking me with him. We were both panting and sweaty as our bodies stayed plastered against each other. No talking was needed or even possible. I was trying to catch my breath and come back to earth. Sex had never been so good. But then my experience was limited. Very limited. I couldn't imagine it got better than this though.

Cruz's hand began to play with my hair casually. I turned my head to look at him, and his eyes were closed. I had always hated that he was so breathtakingly handsome. It made my feelings for him even harder to ignore. I would watch him and be disgusted with myself for doing it. The way he walked, carried himself, the sound of his voice, and that smile of his. All of it was impossible not to notice. All females noticed him.

"Let's go north. What about Memphis?" he said with his eyes closed.

"Memphis? What's in Memphis?" I asked enjoying the freedom to look at him.

"Fucking Graceland is in Memphis," he smirked then.

"You mean you want to see where Elvis lived?" I laughed as I said it.

He tilted his head to look at me and opened one eye. "Hell yeah, I do. That shit is supposed to be tacky. Who wants to miss that?"

I didn't care where we went. I was good with anywhere.

"Okay. Memphis it is then."

"You called your parents?" His question surprised me.

"No," I admitted.

"You better," he sighed. "I'm sure they all know we are to-gether now. Nate would have told them."

"Probably."

He ran a hand over his face and groaned. "Grant is going to kill me."

I didn't respond. Because that was an issue we'd face when this was over. I was on an adventure to run away from the guy who was in bed with me. It was different now. I wasn't trying to change or find a new me. I already had. The girl I was at this moment was nothing like the girl I had been the night he'd called me cold. Now, I just had to ride this as long as it lasted. Because it would end.

"My dad may kill me before your dad. Either way, my life will be short."

That made me smile. "That's a little dramatic," I told him.

He shrugged. "Honestly, it's worth it." His hand ran down my side and squeezed my hip. "Completely fucking worth it."

That wasn't a proclamation of love. I realized that. But it was sweet. I slid a leg over him as I turned until half my body was lying on top of his. Both his eyes opened as I did it. "We're grown," I reminded him. "I think you'll get to live."

He gazed up at me with hooded eyes. "Or you'll kill me before they do. But then death by sex sounds like a good way to go."

I laughed. "I'm just getting up. Not about to attack you."

His hands grabbed my bottom and pulled me on top of him. "Maybe, but putting this hot little body on a man while he's naked and in bed is irresistible."

When he slid into me slowly this time, I moaned loudly and enjoyed being filled one more time before breakfast.

Chapter Twenty-Two

~CRUZ KERRINGTON~

DRIVING ALMOST SIX hours to Memphis today wasn't a good idea. I saw Lila Kate hide a wince when she straddled the bike. We'd fucked like maniacs, and now she was tender. She would claim she wasn't, but I saw it on her face. I shouldn't have pushed for two rounds this morning, but she felt so damn good. It was a clawing need to get inside her again and fuck that—I didn't like wanting someone so badly. Past experience told me a good fuck got a girl out of my system and I moved on. But with Lila Kate that had yet to happen. With her legs tucked behind mine and her body pressed into my back I was already thinking about fucking her again. Jesus, she was like crack to an addict.

I headed toward Birmingham, Alabama. We could stop halfway and rest. Find something to see or do, and then ride the rest of the way. It was just an hour closer than Memphis; she could visit her friend, and it would help control my need to have my dick inside her our entire stop. I needed to find some control.

After eighty minutes on the road she began to squirm, and I

found an exit that had restaurant choices and some shopping. We'd spend time here then head on later when she was ready. Pulling into a parking lot for a barbecue place, I parked and held out my hand to help her off the bike. She made a small wince again.

"Think we might need to stop for the day," I said feeling guilty for her discomfort.

She frowned. "Why?"

I appreciated her trying to be tough, but I had made her sore, and I wasn't going to make her suffer for it. First time I'd ever wished I wasn't riding my damn bike. "You're sore," I pointed out the obvious. "Let's eat, walk around some. Shop. See how you feel later."

"I will be fine," she argued.

I ignored that. "Hungry?"

"Yes, and this place smells great."

We headed inside and I forced myself not to put my hands on her. Touching her all the time was not good. This was temporary. No need acting like it was more than that. We were both enjoying the trip.

Her phone began ringing just before we walked in the door and she stopped to pull it out of her pocket. When she lifted her eyes to me, they were apologetic as she put the phone to her ear. "Hey, Mom."

I'd told her to call her parents more than once. She hadn't listened.

Her mother was talking, and Lila Kate's face went pale before she whispered. "Oh, no. When?"

Now I was worried. She began chewing on her thumbnail. "Yes, he is."

"I'm not sure," she looked back at me. "Where are we?"

"About one hour south of Montgomery, Alabama," I told her.

She repeated that to her mother. "No . . . on his motorcycle,"

I could see her cringe as she said it.

"Yes. We will drive there now," she said. "I'll see you later. And Mom, I'm so sorry."

"I love you, too."

When she ended the call, tears filled her eyes. "My grandmother passed away in the middle of the night. Mom's sending my grandfather's jet to pick me up in Montgomery. They're already in California. My grandfather called Mom at three this morning to tell her. She and Dad got on a plane shortly after and left."

This was the last thing I expected for her to say. "God, Lila, I'm so sorry."

She nodded. "Me too. For my grandfather's sake. She was never there you know. Her mind has been gone for so many years. It's a miracle she lived so long. But Kiro has spent my entire life at her side. They stopped touring because he hated being away from her. Their whole story is just heartbreaking. My mom never got to know her. Her brain has been damaged since Mom was a baby."

I knew their story. It had made the headlines when it was revealed that Kiro Manning's wife Emily was in fact still alive. The world had thought she'd died in that accident. But he'd kept her safe from the media. They had even made a movie called "Kiro's Emily" about ten years ago that had been a box office hit. Kiro hadn't didn't want the movie made at first, but the interview he did for Rolling Stones magazine said that he had changed his mind. He wanted the world to know his Emily. What she had been like. How amazing she was. She deserved it.

I walked Lila back to my bike and helped her on. I put the helmet on her head and wished there was more I could do. Anything else. Something to help. I dreaded putting her on that jet and watching her leave me. Our time was ending sooner than I had expected.

She held onto me tighter than before. My throat felt thick.

There was fucking emotion there I didn't understand. That I didn't want. This had been a way to protect her, get her out of my system, and move on. For both of us. But one night wasn't enough. I was selfish. Her grandmother had just passed away. But dammit this sucked.

The ride to Montgomery airport was too fast. Our time together was ending. This small bubble we had was about to burst. I'd head back home and face the heat with Dad. Do what the hell I was supposed to. She'd return, and it would be like before. We weren't going to pick up where we left off. That would make this more than a fling. That would make the motherfucking lump in my throat mean something.

Hurting Lila Kate was inevitable for me. If I did it later, it would hurt more. Sooner was best. Sooner would help us both move on. I'd never be the guy she needed. But damn if I'd expected it to hurt me too.

We had pulled into the airport before the private jet had arrived. I wanted to say something that made this all easier. That made the ache in my chest go away. That made that sad look in her eyes disappear. But I had nothing.

She climbed off the bike, and I got her things from the saddlebag. Then I turned to her. "Wasn't expecting our journey to end so soon," I said trying to smile.

"Me neither."

I could see the question there. The uncertainty. She wanted to know if this was it for us. But she wouldn't ask. And I couldn't say the words. Even if I needed to, I couldn't.

"Tell your parents and grandfather I'm sorry for their loss." Her eyes lost their light. She had wanted me to say more than a simple generic condolence. I felt like a giant asshole.

"Thanks," she whispered. "For everything." Then she took her bag and walked away. I watched her leave. I wanted to run after her and say something more. To try to make her smile. But that would only make this worse. Instead, I waited until she entered the building. Then I climbed on my bike and headed back south. Back to Rosemary Beach.

Chapter Twenty-Three

♥ LILA KATE ♥

I WAS NUMB. The flight to LA and the ride to my grand-father's house in Beverly Hills had all been a blur. When the limo that had picked me up at the airport parked in front of his mansion, I realized I didn't even remember getting in the limo.

I grabbed the single bag I had with me and stepped out when the driver opened my car door. I hadn't been to see Kiro in about six months. He'd visited us, but I hadn't been here. When I was a kid I visited more often. I stayed a week with him in the summer. I had good memories of this place.

My mother came to the front door and walked out to greet me. I climbed the stairs and hoped she wasn't too upset over my riding around on a motorcycle with Cruz. She had her dad to be worried about. I didn't need to add to her stress. I knew I'd never get on Cruz's bike again.

He'd just let me go. No promises. Nothing. He'd just let it end. That quickly. My chest ached, and I felt guilty it was over a guy. My grandfather was suffering. I should be more concerned about him.

"How is he?" I asked as I hugged her.

She squeezed me. "He's sad. Mom has been gone for a long time. The woman he knew. But now even the little that he had of her is gone. It's going to be tough on him."

"Was she sick?"

"No. Her heart just stopped. With the damage her brain had endured, the doctor says it's a miracle she lived as long as she did. But Daddy made sure she had the best care. And he was always here. I think she lived for him."

Their story was so tragic. When I stepped back, I looked at her. "How upset is Dad?"

"About Cruz?"

I nodded.

"He's not happy," she said with a small shrug. "But you're a grown woman. What can he do? It was your decision to make."

I agreed, but I didn't think Daddy would agree.

"He won't bring it up in there. For now, this is about Kiro and Emily."

"Who all is here?"

"Right now, it's just Dean and us. Nan, Cope, Mase, Reese, Rush and Blaire are all on their way."

Mom looked at the backpack on my shoulder. "What happened to your luggage?"

"I left it all at Nate's."

She sighed. "To run off on Cruz Kerrington's bike."

"Yes."

She didn't say more. I hadn't even been gone a week, and everything that had happened made it seem like it had been so much longer.

"Can I say one thing?" Mom asked.

"Of course."

She reached out and touched my cheek. "You are kind, loving, generous, patient, and beautiful. You deserve something special."

"Mom, you got a fairytale. Not everyone finds those."

She titled her head to the side and smiled. "No, Lila Kate. Not everyone is patient enough to wait for it."

She kissed my cheek then took my arm, and we walked up the stairs and into the house. I would ponder what she said later. Maybe she was right. Maybe it wasn't that I wouldn't get a fairytale. Just that I had wanted it from the wrong person.

The house smelled like cigars. It had all my life. I'd heard Rush once say it was better than the marijuana smell it had in his youth. We walked through the large entrance down the left hall where what Kiro called the game room was located. Large black leather sofas, massive flat screens—as in three of them—a pool table and a large bar were in the room. Sitting on the corner of the sofa was my grandfather, Kiro Manning. He was older now, but he was still a legend. His name was well known. He had a cigar in one hand and a bottle of whiskey in the other. His slender frame was tall, and he was covered in tattoos. Even retired and a grandfather he still resembled a rocker.

He lifted his red-rimmed eyes as we entered and smiled at the sight of me. He'd been crying at some point. "My Lila Kate," he said his voice raspy from years of drugs, smoking and alcohol.

"Hey," I said as I made my way over to him. It was no secret he'd been furious when my father got my mother pregnant. My mother wasn't his only child but she was his favorite. Because she had been the child Emily gave him. My birth could have killed my mother. That had terrified him. But my mom often said he'd spent my lifetime making that up to me. I knew he loved me more than his other grandchildren. He was very blunt about it. But I also knew it was only because I was a part of Emily.

He held open his arms still holding the alcohol and cigar. I bent down and hugged him tightly. "I love you," I whispered.

"Not as much as I love you, pretty girl," which had always been his response. "Heard you took off on a bike with a Kerrington. Guess you got a little of your Granddaddy's wild oats in you after all."

I tensed hoping my dad hadn't heard him. "Um, I guess," I said as quietly as I could.

That made him laugh. I was glad he could laugh but this wasn't something to laugh about. "Gonna give that daddy of yours a little hard time. He needs it."

Of all the things for him to want to talk about this wasn't one of them.

"Daddy be nice. She's already nervous about talking to Grant about all this," Mom interjected.

I closed my eyes and winced. When I stood up Kiro winked at me. "You're grown girl. It's okay."

I turned my head slowly to look at my dad who was standing at the bar with his arms crossed over his chest and a frown on his face. "She's better than Cruz Kerrington," my dad said.

"And my Harlow was better than Grant Carter. My sweet baby girl was swept off her feet by someone who had a reputation as a player. Seems it turned out all right," Kiro said before taking a pull off his cigar.

Dad only grunted.

I tried thinking of something to change the subject when footsteps sounded down the hall. Then I heard the voices. Kiro's other two kids were here with their spouses. I knew my Uncle Mase's voice anywhere. And when he is arguing with my Aunt Nan it feels like a family gathering.

"I'm not taking the blue room, Mase. Shove it up your ass. I want the gold one near the back elevator. I always prefer that one. Don't argue with me," Aunt Nan said in her high-pitched annoyed tone.

"Give me another fucking bottle. I'm gonna need it," Kiro grumbled.

He and my Aunt Nan didn't have the best relationship, but Mom said it was good compared to the way it had once been.

When the four entered the room. Kiro held up his bottle. "I'm fucking mourning. Don't start this shit in here."

Nan looked ashamed, and Mase nodded. "Sorry. I was just getting her riled up out of boredom."

Kiro lifted one shoulder in a shrug. "Understood."

"I'm so sorry, Kiro," Reese, my Uncle Mase's wife said as she walked away from the others toward Kiro. "You go ahead and mourn, and I'll keep these two in check."

"Still ain't figured out how the fuck you scored that one," Kiro said pointing with his bottle toward Reese while looking at Mase.

"Me neither," Mase replied then sank down on the sofa across from Kiro. "Pass the whiskey."

Chapter Twenty-Four

~CRUZ KERRINGTON~

THE SMELL OF flowers. I hated the overpowering smell as much as I hated funerals. They depressed me. I shouldn't have to be here. I didn't know Emily Manning. Sure, I knew Lila Kate but I wouldn't expect her to come to my grandmother's funeral. Hell, I wouldn't go if I could get away with it. Once someone was dead it as done. Why have a big ass depressing funeral?

I wanted my ashes taken out a few miles into the Gulf and scattered. No songs, no flowers, and no fucking tears. I loosened the collar on my shirt some and sighed. My dad had been adamant that I was going. We all were. The whole damn family was here. As was every other family in Rosemary Beach that we were close to.

"We are going for Grant, Harlow and Lila Kate!" my dad had roared when I bitched about not seeing a reason to attend this funeral.

The truth was, I had tried to get Lila out of my head for the past three days and it wasn't working. All I could see was Lila. When I'd had another girl pressed up against the wall of my condo last night, I'd had Lila Kate's face in my head. I didn't want to see her this soon. I was still working her out of my system. I even pointed out to my father that they may be having a funeral for me once Grant Carter got his hands on me. Dad had told me I'd asked for it.

"There's Nate," my mother whispered. "Go apologize."

"For what?" I asked confused. I hadn't done shit to Nate.

She grabbed my arm like I was still eight years old. "For taking Lila Kate without a word. That's what for."

I wasn't apologizing to him for that. "No."

Her nails bit into my skin. "Now."

I wasn't apologizing, but I'd walk over there and say something to him to let her think I did before she grabbed me by my ear and hauled me to him.

"Fine," I muttered and her hand released me as soon as I headed in his direction.

Apologize to Nate. Seriously? Did they even know Nate Finlay? As if this wasn't something he would have done. Jesus. They were all being dramatic as hell. I didn't kidnap her. She went willingly.

Nate was also dressed in a suit, and Bliss stood beside him looking stunning in a black dress with her hair pulled up off her shoulders. "Hey," I said as they turned to see me approaching.

Nate did a lift of his chin.

"You seen Lila Kate?" I asked.

"Yeah. Why? You got your bike with you?" Nate smirked as he said it.

"No, smartass. I just don't see her."

"She's gone to get a drink. Been talking to everyone and her mouth got dry."

I nodded. Good. I'd have time to get back out of sight before she returned. "Y'all here long?"

"We came in last night. Stayed at Dean's. Heading out in the morning," Nate replied. Dean was his grandfather. Kiro Manning's best friend.

"I'm headed out soon as this is over," I said. "Good to see you again, Bliss. I think I've been over here long enough for my mother to think I've apologized sufficiently. I'll leave you to it."

Nate grinned. "Apologized, huh? I think I'd like that apology."

Bliss giggled. "Nate leave him alone. It's good to see you again, Cruz." She started to say more, then paused and smiled at something over my shoulder. "There they are," she added.

I glanced back without thinking and my eyes locked on Lila Kate. She was stunning. Her dark hair was curled loosely and brushed her shoulders. The midnight blue dress she was wearing hugged her curves so damn sweetly I had a hard time looking away.

"Should I get him? Or do you think she wants him to stay with her?" Bliss asked.

Get who?

"Leave it. She seems to want him with her," Nate replied.

I tore my gaze off Lila Kate to see a tall blond guy with his hand possessively on her back. His expression was serious as he listened to something she was saying. Who the fuck was that?

"Who is with her?" I asked since they obviously knew.

"That's Eli, my best friend," Bliss said with a pleased smile.

"How does she know him?" Lila Kate wasn't one to bond with someone fast.

"They had been spending some time together before you rode in on your bike and took off with her," Nate replied. He was amused. He knew why I was asking and he was fucking amused.

"She wanted to go with me," I told him turning to glare at his smug expression.

He nodded. "Yeah, she did. But now," he tilted his chin up toward Lila Kate. "She wants Eli. Lesson learned fast I'd say."

"What the fuck does that mean?" I snarled taking a step

toward him.

Nate didn't back away. But then I didn't expect him to. He took a step in my direction. His expression went cold. Hard. "It means Eli is a good guy. The staying kind. That's what it fucking means," Nate's voice was low as he said the words.

"She barely knows him," I argued.

"But she knows you enough, now doesn't she," he shot back.

We were at a funeral. That should be why I stopped and walked away. But it wasn't. It was because Nate was right. She did know me. I could have parked my bike and gone with her. That's what a good guy would have done. But I'd fucked her, dropped her off and driven away. As I let myself think about it I had to admit that might have been the coldest thing I'd ever done. And I'd done some pretty cruel shit. I turned my gaze back to Lila Kate and Eli. He was whispering something to her and she smiled. The smile wasn't the radiant one I knew.

It was sad. Her eyes didn't glow and light up the room like I knew they could. She'd lost someone, and Eli was there with her. That's the kind of guy she needed. I had left her because she needed to move on from me. I just hadn't fucking expected it to happen so fast.

"She deserves more. You know it. Let her have it," Nate's voice annoyed me simply because he was right. I didn't say anything to him. I just walked away. Back to my family. I would get through this damn funeral and leave quietly. I'd forget what happened with Lila and me. Eventually.

As I was walking away I felt her eyes follow me. The best thing to do would be to ignore her but I couldn't. I met her gaze. She didn't smile. She just looked at me with eyes so full of disappointment it burned in my gut. She'd ruined me. Just like I was afraid she would.

Chapter Twenty-Five
♥ LILA KATE ♥

ELI'S HAND HELD mine as I studied the private mausoleum that was for all Slacker Demon members and their family. My grandmother was the first to be buried in it. Kiro had bought it because he said he didn't want to be buried in the ground and he didn't want his Emily in there either. So he'd decided that the best way to rest in eternal peace was a mausoleum with those he loved most.

"I've never seen anyone laid to rest in one of these. Just been to burials," Eli said softly beside me.

"Me neither. It seems easier than watching them sink into the ground doesn't it?"

He nodded. "Yeah, I guess it does."

I focused on my grandfather as his bloodshot eyes stared straight ahead at the marking where Emily had been slid in. He was drinking from another bottle of whiskey. I was concerned he was going to get alcohol poisoning, but my mom said he'd built years of tolerance to the stuff. He'd be fine. His suit covered his tattoos but he still looked like a rocker. It was in his stance, face, the way his hair was still too long for an older man. He would always be Kiro Manning. Even at seventy years old.

"Thanks for staying with me today," I told Eli. I had needed someone. Support. Everyone had been here. They all knew I'd been on Cruz Kerrington's bike and they all saw him completely ignore me. But my grandfather's grief had been more important than my obvious snub from Cruz. I'd gotten what I asked for playing with fire.

"I'm glad I came. Almost didn't. Nate thought I should. I'll have to thank him for that."

Nate had expected this. He knew Cruz as well as I did. We had been a pack once. I needed to thank Nate for bringing Eli. Not that I was going to use Eli as a rebound. But he'd become a good friend. After today, I hoped we would stay in touch. I enjoyed his company. He was strong. Dependable. Kind. The type of man I knew my parents hoped I would find one day.

When my heart finally healed and I moved on, I hoped I would find a fairytale with a guy like Eli. I knew it wouldn't be Eli because his heart was already unavailable. I sympathized with him. Loving someone you will never have is painful.

At least he hadn't suffered humiliation because of it. He'd kept his feelings a secret. Never made the mistake of throwing caution to the wind and hoping it worked.

"Let's go," I said as others began to leave. I knew my grandfather would be here for a while and I wanted him to have his alone time with her.

Eli continued to hold my hand as we walked away. I knew the Kerrington's were to my left. I could see Woods and Della from the corner of my eye. But I didn't turn to them. I just couldn't bring myself to. I walked on with my head down. Eli led me to the limo that was waiting for the family.

"Where are you going?" I asked him.

He nodded toward the limo behind this one. "To Dean's with Nate and Bliss."

Being with Nate and Bliss wasn't easy on him. I knew that without asking. "Come with me," I said.

He smiled like he understood why and could read my thoughts. "Thanks."

I moved all the way down to the last seat. "You saved me today. I should be thanking you."

He moved in behind me and sat with his thigh pressing mine. The warmth from his body, the smell of his cologne all made me feel soothed. Like I wasn't alone. I remembered this from our one night together. I knew the difference now, between good drunk sex with no strings and sex with a man your heart wants. It's on two different playing fields.

"You were beautiful today. He's an idiot, and from the way he watched your every move he knows it."

I jerked my head around and looked up at Eli. "What?"

He gave me a half smile. "Cruz Kerrington. He couldn't keep his eyes off you. I never met him nor was I introduced, but I know guys like him. I can spot them. He was also completely obvious. No one else there glared at me like they'd enjoy ripping my limbs off my body."

That didn't make sense. I shook my head. "You misunderstood. He was forced to come here. I know his parents. He was glaring because he was angry this took away from his play time." The disgust was obvious in my voice. So was the hurt.

"I may not be an asshole. But I am a man. I know what they're thinking. I can read one. And that guy was not happy about you being with me. He also wanted to get you alone and get his hands on you. Honestly, Lila, you are beautiful. Today you were stunning. I had a hard time keeping my eyes off you."

It felt nice. No, it felt more than nice to hear a good-looking man say that to me. I didn't feel beautiful or stunning. "Thank you," I said unsure of how else to respond. Then I said what I was thinking. "I wish . . . I wish I'd met you at another time. A time when our hearts weren't so confused. Maybe we would have had a chance."

His hand slipped over mine, and he kept it there. "When you left I realized something. My heart isn't where I thought it was. Bliss had become a habit. All I knew. No one had made enough of an impact on me to move her from my heart. But you . . . you made me forget. Showed me that there was more. That I could feel something for someone else," he paused then his fingers slid around mine. "My heart's ready, Lila. I'll just be patient until yours is."

Wow . . . that was not something I'd expected to hear. "Our last night together you were upset over being the best man," I reminded him.

He shrugged. "A habit. A habit that shook me up and showed me how my heart had changed. I realized I'd moved on when I found out you were gone. That . . . that shook me more than the damn wedding shit. I was over it and completely focused on you. I don't even get a twinge when I see them kiss now. You got me over it. I wish I could do the same for you."

Here was this wonderful man telling me he wanted more. He was ready to move on with me. He wanted to be with me. He made himself available. And as beautiful as it all sounded, my heart was still aching over Cruz. I was either the stupidest female on planet Earth or the unluckiest. Possibly both.

"I need time," I said to him because I wanted a fairy tale. I believed that Eli was that kind of guy. He was secure, solid, beautiful. All the things my father was, Rush Finlay was, my Uncle Mase and Uncle Cope were. I wanted a man like them.

"I'm really patient," he replied.

Even the tone of his voice was soothing. It didn't make my heart flip or butterflies take flight in my stomach, but it made me feel safe. I rested my head on his shoulder. His arm went around me and we sat there like that in silence while we waited on the rest of the family.

Chapter Twenty-Six

~CRUZ KERRINGTON~

"DID YOU FUCK her?" Blaze, my nineteen-year-old brother asked dropping down onto the other end of the sectional sofa in the den that my mom referred to as "the boys' den." It was on the bottom floor of our three-story home and had everything teenage boys could possibly need. Even a mini gym with weights. I had come down here as soon as we got home to avoid the rest of the family.

"I'm ignoring that," I replied not taking my attention from the baseball game I was watching.

Blaze chuckled. "That means yes. Goddamn! She's so fucking hot."

Fury crawled all over me. "If you want to live you'll shut the hell up," I warned him. I didn't want anyone knowing about what we had done, but I also didn't want my brother thinking about Lila Kate and sex in the same damn thought.

"What's your deal? Jesus, relax. Lila Kate is smoking hot. I'd give my left nut to fuck her."

I moved then. Fast. Without thought. I pinned Blaze to the

sofa with my hand around his throat. He was an inch, maybe two taller than me but he was lankier. His muscles were slenderer. I outweighed him. I was also two years older. "Shut your mother-fucking mouth. Do you understand me you stupid little dipshit?"

He nodded unable to breathe so I eased my hold on his neck. Then glared at him one last time before moving off him and taking my spot back. "Go away," I told him as I settled back again.

I could see him rubbing his neck. Damn dramatic. He finally stood up, and I was so relieved I almost sighed. I just wanted to be alone.

"If you love her then you aren't doing a good job of showing her. That's all I'm saying." After the words had left his mouth, he turned and ran from the room and back up the stairs.

"I don't love her," I said to no one. But I needed to say it. Get it out. "I don't love anyone. Love isn't for me." I kept talking to the empty room.

The image of Lila Kate standing at the funeral. Her soft tanned back so perfect and bare in the dress she was wearing it made my fingers itch to touch it. To feel it's silky texture. If Eli Fucking Hardy had laid one hand on that back, I wouldn't have been responsible for my actions. But he hadn't. He'd been the good guy. He didn't touch her body. He only held her hand.

She'd seemed to need that support. I fought against the jealousy eating at me that I wasn't the one there beside her. It was my choice that I wasn't. I was suffering for her benefit.

Footsteps on the stairs this time alerted me I was about to be interrupted yet again by a family member. I lay my head back and closed my eyes as I sighed with annoyance. "Can't you all just leave me alone?" I growled in frustration as the next nosey ass member of my family entered the room.

"I'll just be a minute. I need to say something. Then I won't bother you again," Lila Kate's voice had my head snapping back up. What the fuck was she doing here?

She was dressed in a white sundress that showed too much of her skin. I soaked it in. The sight of her. All that perfect softness. Here in my house. Why?

"Blaze said you were down here and I could come see you a moment. He was leaving to meet your parents for lunch at the club. I didn't mean to bother you," she paused and looked at the game on the television. "I see you're busy watching something. I'll be quick."

She walked over to me stopping only a few feet away. "I didn't make a mistake. I knew what I was doing. I expected this of you. I didn't expect anything more. I chose to go with you, sleep with you, allow myself to enjoy being with you. That was all on me. I will deal with the memories. The heartbreak. All of it because I asked for it. At first, I thought I was stupid. I cursed my bad decisions. But . . . I am thankful I did it. I let you hurt me. But we had a moment. I now know how that feels. How you . . . feel. I don't regret it. I don't regret you. I'll move on. Go another way. I won't ever bother you again. Life will return to the way it was before." She stopped then and smiled. It was a sweet, sad smile. It made my fucking knees feel weak, and I was sitting down.

"It was less than forty-eight hours, but it had been fun. Exciting. And I will always be glad I did it. Thank you, Cruz Kerrington," she said as she closed the distance between us and bent down to press a kiss to my lips. "Goodbye," she whispered against them. Then she stood up and walked toward the stairs.

My lips were still tingling from the excitement of her touch. My body hummed from the scent of her body. Letting her go seemed impossible. I was off the sofa and behind her so quickly I didn't have time to think this through. My hands grabbed her waist, and I pressed her up against the wall squeezing her under my touch. There were a million things I wanted to say. But I said none of them.

I kissed her this time, and I did it right. No fucking peck on the lips. I claimed her mouth. Tasted her sweetness. Got drunk on the nectar that was Lila Kate. I'd craved this since I left her. I'd dreamed about it. Tried to get it out of my system with another woman. None of it worked. This was the only way to cure my craving.

Her hands tangled in my hair and my hands moved up to feel the heaviness of her breasts. I laid my hand over her heart, and the pounding of it made my heart soar. I did this to her. She wanted it just like I did. We were like fucking explosives. There had never been another woman to make me react this way. Why couldn't we just make it last longer? Enjoy it until it fizzled out.

When her hands touched my chest and pushed me back firmly, I was dazed.

"That's enough," she panted and slipped away from my body to free herself from where I'd pinned her.

"We were just getting started," I replied my own voice hoarse from lack of oxygen.

She shook her head. "No, Cruz. My kiss was a goodbye. That kiss was closure." While I was trying to wrap my head around what she'd just said she walked away. Left me there. Just like that. No tears. Nothing.

Would I have felt better if she'd cried? I didn't want to hurt her. I wanted to lock myself in a room with her and never leave again. But I didn't want to hurt her.

She'd shown me her emotions before. On Bourbon Street, I'd seen it. All of it. I knew that her heart was soft. That her tears flowed easily. So, that meant the woman that just walked out of here was one thing . . . what I had made her. She wasn't cold. She was finished. I had shown her just how badly I could hurt her and she'd seen that I wasn't worth it. She knew she deserved more.

Her smell clung to my skin. My body ached from the loss of her in my arms. But more than that my soul knew I'd just pushed away the one thing that had ever woken it up. Shook it. I had lost the woman that had shown me what fire felt like.

I sank onto the chair behind me. Buried my head in my hands. It was done. We'd had our small moment. I'd meant to show her how I was bad for her. How I would ruin her. I had been preserving us both. But in the end, I was the one that would be completely ruined.

Chapter Twenty-Seven

♥ LILA KATE ♥

THE SPACE WAS perfect. It would grow with me. With my dance classes. I could see a future here. I had the money to start it. I'd buy this place, all the equipment, and start advertising. Sure, I'd wanted to find an adventure two weeks ago but now an adventure would always remind me of Cruz. He'd been my ultimate adventure.

I had almost let his presence in this town run me out. When I admitted to myself I was looking at dance studios outside of Rosemary Beach because I was trying to avoid Cruz, I had begun my search here. It only made sense for me to start my first studio in a town where I knew everyone and move further out later to expand. I didn't plan on staying here forever. But for now, it made sense. My need for adventure had been sucked out. It had been fleeting. I'd had a little too much adventure in one weeks' time to last me a few years.

The door opened behind me, and Ophelia Finlay stood there looking as glamourous as she always did. "I called you three times," she told me as if I hadn't seen the missed calls on my phone.

"I've been busy," I replied.

She sighed loudly. "You won't even consider it? I'd be an amazing roommate."

Ophelia had heard from her mother that I was buying a condo and starting my own dance studio. Word travels fast when your mothers are best friends. She was taking a "break" from college this year because she needed new direction or something of that nature. It was very Ophelia.

"I wasn't not considering it. I don't doubt you'd be a good roommate. I just needed to make sure this was what I was going to do," I turned in a circle looking at the building. "This is it though. This is the place."

Ophelia nodded. "It'll make a good studio. Great location."

I pointed at the ceiling. "My apartment will be up there. I'm buying the building. I need to save money, and living where I work makes sense."

That got a frown. "You're living here?"

I nodded. "Yep."

"What's it look like up there?"

I shrugged. "A very large loft. Exposed beams, very open. Not really your kind of place." Which is why I hadn't answered her calls.

"Will you have early classes?" she asked, still not looking pleased.

"Eight in the morning," I replied.

Her determination to be my new roommate looked like it was fading fast. "Oh."

That's what I thought. This would be my world. My work and my loft. I didn't imagine that would appeal to anyone else.

"Can I see it?" she asked hopefully.

"Sure. Let's go," I replied. "This way." I led the way to the back door that was painted blue. I'd change that. It opened to the stairs that went up to the loft. There were exactly twenty-five stairs. When we reached the top, there was no door. I would work on that, too.

The four thousand square foot area was almost completely open. The only privacy was a bathroom to the far left and the spiral staircase that led to yet another loft area that would be my bedroom. The kitchen was complete and all stainless steel. Even the countertops were stainless. It was all very industrial.

"Is there a second bedroom?" she asked taking in the area.

"No. The original owner was a single man. But if you're really interested there is enough room. We can build walls to that back corner by the bathroom, and you'd have a sufficient size bedroom. We will have to share the bathroom though."

She studied it walking around and taking in the view over the business area of Rosemary. It was small and a quaint street with shops. The outside of all the shops were all very Southern coastal, and it felt comfortable. Very different from the area where we had lived as kids. Finally, she turned to me and smiled. "Let's do it."

If this had been Phoenix Finlay, I would have said absolutely not. But Ophelia I could live with. Besides, the rental income would pay the utilities on this place. Business-wise it just made sense.

"I'll have Dad get some workers up here to get you a room put up as soon as I sign the paperwork on this place."

She was grinning brightly. "How long do you think that will be?"

"Later this week."

She clapped her hands excitedly. "This is going to be so much fun!"

I hoped so. "You want a job? Because I'll need office help once I open the studio up."

"Sure! Why the hell not? Can we just take the rent out of my paycheck?"

"That would be fine with me."

We talked some more before Ophelia left to tell her mother her plans. I went over and pulled myself up to sit on the bar in the kitchen. I could make a life here. It wasn't in the wealthy part of Rosemary Beach where the big houses were and the club was located. It was right beside it, but it felt separate. I wasn't leaving town but I was starting a new life in this town.

My phone rang and echoed in the large empty space. I glanced at it. It was Eli. Smiling, I pressed answer. "Hello."

"How's the place look?" he asked. I had told him I was coming to check it out today in a text message I'd sent him last night.

"Perfect. I think it's going to be perfect."

"Damn. I was hoping you'd think it sucked and come to Sea Breeze to shop around." He was teasing but I knew that he'd also be pleased if that did happen.

"You could always come to Rosemary Beach," I replied.

He was quiet for a moment. "Don't tempt me."

I wondered if he would actually do that. Maybe a fresh start for him was what he needed. "I wouldn't complain if you did," I added

He chuckled and added, "You'd be hard to say no to. But I have a job. Can't just up and run away."

He had a point. "I know. Wanted to clarify if you needed an adventure I would be happy to be the beginning of yours." I'd been teasing, but he had gone quiet.

I chewed on my lip nervously. Maybe I shouldn't have said that. We didn't talk about that night much. I wasn't sure if he remembered asking me if he was the beginning of my adventure. I waited for him to say something and worried the whole time he was silent.

"I might consider it if we could have another go at sex on the beach. I think about it a lot. Wish to God I hadn't been so damn drunk."

After Cruz, I wasn't ready for sex with anyone. I wanted to be one day. But for now, I just couldn't. In one week, I'd had sex with two different men. That had been one hell of an adventure.

"One day. If the time is right," I said softly while images of Cruz and the things we'd done played in my head. My heart ached along with them.

"I don't want to just be the beginning of your adventure Lila. I want to be the end."

Chapter Twenty-Eight

~Cruz Kerrington~

M Y HEAD WAS fucked. I was at work doing what my father had asked me to do. Not because he'd asked but because I was so damn fucked in the head I needed something to distract me. And other women's vaginas weren't working.

"Cruz, you look so much like your father at that age I had a flashback. I was a waitress again and there was the boss. You're all dressed up in your Kerrington Club polo. I know Woods is proud to have you here with him," Blaire Finlay said as she walked into the dining room with my mother and Harlow Carter, Lila's mother.

"He's his father's twin. In everything including attitude," my mother said with a smile.

"Don't tell him you said that," I drawled knowing he wouldn't want to hear that I acted like him at all.

Blaire laughed, and the three of them walked past me. My mother paused to squeeze my arm gently. Harlow was quiet. She didn't talk loudly like the others or draw attention to herself. She was proper, beautiful, looked nothing even close to her age, and all I could see was Lila Kate twenty years from now. The man that caught her would be one lucky son of a bitch.

Annoyed at my train of thought, I walked down the hall toward my father's office where I'd been headed when those three had arrived. I used to love coming to this office. It meant I got to see my dad. He'd set me up on his desk and let me play with the small golf toy that was on it. I'd watch the flat screen on his wall and observe him as he worked. I wanted to be just like him.

My, how times had changed.

The door to Dad's office opened and he stepped out before I reached him. His gaze immediately locked on me. "Good. You're on time. I'm having a lunch meeting with Captain—you remember Blaire Finlay's brother—and his daughter Emmeline is with him. She's being groomed to take over the restaurant franchise here in Rosemary Beach. I think having you there will make her feel more comfortable since you're closer in age."

Lunch meeting. Fan-fucking-tastic. "I know Emmeline, and she goes by Emmy. Or at least she did two years ago when I spoke to her at an event held here for something or another."

Dad nodded. "Good. Franny, Captain's oldest daughter oversees the franchises in Alabama and Tennessee. Emmeline is being trained to take over the Florida and Georgia franchises. She won't be ready until she graduates college, but Captain starts them young preparing them. Like I should have done with you. Smart businessman." Dad said as he kept walking expecting me to keep up.

"Are we eating here?" I asked hoping the answer was no. I wasn't in the mood to deal with the crowd in there.

"No. Captain's place."

"Why are we meeting with him exactly?"

"Because we need another restaurant at the club. The poolside grill and the main dining room aren't enough. Not anymore. It's time we expanded."

"So you're going to put one of Captain's restaurants in the club?"

"Possibly. It sounds like a good idea. We will see what plays out."

Dad's new Dodge Ram was parked out front and a valet had it already started for us. We climbed in and headed off the club property toward the business part of Rosemary Beach where the stores, eating, shopping and touristy shit was located. I didn't say much, just watched the town pass by. Wondered about Lila Kate because that was my new habit I couldn't shake.

"Talked to Lila Kate lately?" Dad asked as if he could read my mind.

I shook my head no.

"Then you don't know about her buying that place," he said, and my ears perked up.

"What?"

Dad stopped at one of the three traffic lights in town and pointed to a two-story storefront at the corner of the main street. "That one right there on the end. Grant said she bought it. She's opening a dance studio."

I studied the coastal pale blue building. Large windows lined the bottom floor and the second floor had the hurricane shutters that were so damn popular around here. "That can't be cheap," I said wondering what the hell she was thinking.

"It wasn't. But she has a trust fund from Kiro. She's got a good business head. Instead of living off the money she's using it to make more. To build something."

I could hear the admiration in his tone. I knew she was fucking special. He didn't have to nail that point home. I got it. That was why I pushed her away. It had worked too well.

Dad pulled the truck into the front of Captain's place in Rosemary Beach, and I climbed out still looking back at the place that was now Lila's. She wasn't leaving town. That felt good. Like I could take a deep breath. Not that where she lived mattered, but I wanted her here. As fucked up as that was.

"Listen, pay attention, and be polite. Talk to Emmeline. Don't act like an ass."

I smirked. "When have I ever been an ass to a female?"

"Numerous times, Cruz. Numerous."

Scowling, I followed him inside and the smell of seafood hit me. I hadn't been here in a long time, but it was good food. I should get out more often. Wouldn't hurt me to come into this part of town.

"Woods, Cruz, good to see both of you," Captain Kipling said as he shook dad's hand then mine. "When did you turn into a man?" he joked then slapped me on the back.

Emmy walked up beside him and smiled at me. It wasn't the kind of polite business smile I was expecting either. She was older and in the past two years she'd matured. She also knew it. Her long blonde hair and bright green eyes were a striking combination against the sun-kissed tan of her skin.

"Hello, Cruz," her eyes sparkled with mischief as she said my name.

"Emmy," I replied with a nod. "Good to see you."

"While y'all get seated I'll take Cruz with me to get the laptop you need, Daddy. I can show him around in the back."

Captain and my dad were already doing the chummy talk, and he just nodded. My dad gave me a warning glare before walking away. This didn't seem like a good idea. Did those two not see the way Emmy had looked at me? Were they that blind? She was not thinking about fucking business.

"You're getting prepped to take over the club Dad tells me," she said walking so close to me her arm brushed against me.

"Yeah," I replied.

"I'll be in town more often getting to know this place. For the summer, I'm here to work. Until I go back to UT in the fall. We should do something," her voice had dropped to a sultry tone. Shit.

"Not sure what you're thinking, but we'll potentially be working together. Don't think we need to cross any lines."

She moved closer then stepped in front of me to open a door and led me inside. I was in the room and realized it was an office before she closed the door behind her. "What's wrong with having a little fun? It will make working together more enjoyable."

Her hand touched my arm and ran up it as she stepped closer to me. "I've always had a crush on you. But I think all the girls have."

Fuck me. What the hell was I supposed to do with this? Normally, I'd dive right into this invitation, but the timing was off here. My head was messed up, and Emmy wasn't someone my dad would be okay with me pissing off.

"Look, as tempting as that may be, we have to work together. I'm sure you're well aware of my reputation. I don't want any friction between us."

She giggled then and moved in front of me. Her chest almost touched mine. "I'm not looking for a relationship, Cruz. I just want some fun."

If I could see past Lila Kate's face, I might take her up on that. But damn, I couldn't use Emmy that way. I'd have to close my eyes and pretend. The last girl I was with two nights before, I'd actually called her Lila. It hadn't gone over well.

Although if someone could get me over my Lila obsession, it would save me. "I'll be honest with you. I'm hung up on someone right now. Working through it. Getting over it. But I am just not there yet."

Emmy bit her lower lip seductively and then finally pressed her tits against my chest. "I can help you with that."

Why did this shit always happen to me? "Not sure that's a good idea," I argued, but my words didn't sound very convincing. She felt nice. I was a guy and I would be lying if I said I didn't enjoy it.

"Give me a chance. Just one taste and you'll see," she whispered and then her hand slid up the inside of my thigh and cupped my dick. Holy shit!

"You get me hard and I'll have to walk out there with a boner. That won't go over well with either of our fathers."

"If I give you a boner I can fix it for you."

This time I laughed. "Trust me, babe. We don't have time for that."

She moved her hand away while I was already getting semi hard. "When you do have time . . . I'm great at sucking cock."

I was still stuck on her words when she moved away and picked up a thin laptop. "Let's get to that meeting. I'm starving," she said as she shot me a wicked grin, then swung her hips as she headed back out the door.

I could possibly do this. Enjoy her. Have some fun. She was not the good girl I had assumed. Emmy Kipling was naughty. Must be that college girl gone wild thing. I was considering it and relaxed a little bit by the time we had joined our fathers.

Emmy suddenly became all business and was charming and intelligent. She knew a lot about the place and made both men laugh as she spoke about shit that was funny. I didn't talk as much, but I engaged to keep my father happy.

Just when I was good with this, and I felt like it was going to be okay. At least, not nearly as bad as I had assumed when Dad said we had to come to this meeting. I began to smile and do a little flirting of my own. I winked at Emmy when our fathers were busy discussing something else and she gave me a smile that promised something later. Something I was getting ready to accept. Then I felt it. Warm heat. Tingles. Lifting my eyes, they locked with the ones I couldn't get out of my head.

Lila Kate stood there with a to go order in her hands. Her eyes were on me. The hurt was obvious and seeing it there sliced through my chest. I was a bastard.

Chapter Twenty-Nine

♥ LILA KATE ♥

I DROPPED MY food on the counter of my kitchen and screamed in frustration. I hated him. I hated Cruz Kerrington. I hated him. Jerking open a cabinet, I got out a glass and filled it with ice water. His stupid grin in my head as he winked at Emmeline Kipling. She was what, nineteen? God, he was a pig.

If she let him near her she was stupid. Stupid like me. I groaned at the thought and opened my bag to get out the food that no longer looked appealing. There were other places I could have eaten today. Why did I have to go there? Why did I have to see that?

I sat down on one of the colorful barstools that had just arrived yesterday. This place was so industrial I had added all the color and art I could. I liked the way it was turning out. The stools were painted by an artist in town and each one had a different crazy artistic face painted on the back.

I stared at the crab claws in front of me as I forced one into my mouth. I had to eat. I'd been working downstairs all day and I was still a good month away from opening the place. I took a drink of my water and then looked over at my phone. I hadn't talked to Eli in two weeks. He knew I had bought the place, but I'd been so busy getting moved in I hadn't texted him.

I reached for my phone and decided to change that. We weren't meant to be more than friends but I'd come to enjoy his friendship. We both loved people who didn't love us. He understood.

Moved in. When are you coming to visit? then I pressed send.

Ophelia wasn't moved in yet. Her room was almost completed. She'd gone to LA with Phoenix to visit their grandfather for a week. The place had been quiet. Just me and my dad along with some of his crew who had been working on the room the last few days.

When I'm invited. Was his reply.

I missed him. I missed the trustworthy guy who I could depend on to do what he said he was going to do. He was honest and didn't do things that could hurt others. I wished that Eli had been the one to steal my heart. Seeing Cruz with someone else would be easier if he had.

You're invited. Consider this your official invitation.

Texting him eased the ache I felt in my heart and I began to eat my food and enjoy it. If I could go back and not beg Cruz for the impossible that night on Bourbon Street, I would. I'd take it all back. Give up the memories. People that said they wouldn't trade it even though it hurts were crazy. I would give it up in a heartbeat. I didn't want to think about him.

I wanted to forget it all.

Friday night too soon? Eli texted back.

It's perfect, I replied.

That gave me two days to get this place ready. I would make some plans for us and then enjoy myself. I wouldn't think about Cruz. I wouldn't care what or who he was doing. I would live my life.

I'll start packing.

I laughed at that last text and finished eating.

Things were turning out different than I had imagined but they weren't bad. Not at all. I was excited. Soon I'd own a dance studio. I'd get to teach kids. I'd encourage them to find their love of dance the way I had.

I cleaned up my meal and went downstairs to get back to painting the walls. Dad had offered to do it, but I wanted to know I had done something. This was my place. I liked having my hand in getting it ready to move in.

When I walked in the door, Cruz was standing there looking around. His hands were in his jeans pockets, a look I couldn't quite read on his face. I thought about turning around and running back upstairs but I wasn't twelve. I was an adult and this was my studio.

"Can I help you?" I asked.

His gaze swung to me. He hadn't heard me come in. "Hey."

I didn't respond to that. I just continued silently stare at him.

"About what you saw," he began and I held up a hand to stop him.

"Don't. Please don't come in here and act like you have to explain anything to me. I think I made myself clear at your house. We had closure. It's done. I have painting to do. If you'll excuse me." I walked over to the paint and roller I had left earlier hoping he'd just turn and leave.

"If you've got your fucking closure why did your eyes look so damn hurt? Tell me that, Lila. Tell me why those eyes of yours took my goddamn breath away? Because it sure as hell wasn't fucking closure I saw in them."

I paused and took a deep breath. He was right. But I wasn't going to admit it. "Still just fresh. I'll be over it soon enough."

"When you figure out how to get over it could you fucking

tell me how? Because God knows I need help myself."

I couldn't let him get to me. I couldn't let his words make me weak or think I could ever trust him. That we could ever have anything.

"You were doing just fine," I shot back bending to get the roller and take the top off the paint can.

"Lila, look at me. Jesus, just fucking look at me. Tell me if this looks like a guy who is over it? You saw me flirt. I have been flirting since I was old enough to walk. It means nothing. It's just how I react to women who are flirting with me."

I laughed then shook my head. "Whatever. I do not care. Just go."

He stood there. Not speaking and not moving. I tried to focus on my painting, but it was hard with his eyes watching me. I waited for him to say something more. If he'd just leave this would eventually go away. All of it. I'd gotten a taste. Knew what it felt like and was ready to put it behind me.

"If you didn't care then we could sit down, chat, have a beer. We can't do that, Lila. So yes, you care."

He was right. I hated him being right. If I didn't care there would be no emotion. I'd be fine with a visit. I wouldn't be demanding he leave. I dropped my hands to my side and turned back to face him.

"You're right. I care. But I want to not care. I want to forget it all happened. I want to forget you." The words although they were true sounded much colder and harsher when said aloud. I almost retracted them but I stopped myself. He'd hurt me. If that hurt him then good.

"I don't want to forget," his voice was deep and almost pained. I started to say something to smooth it over but he did as I asked then. He turned and left. After the door closed behind him, the place was once silent again. And I was alone once again.

Chapter Thirty

~ELI HARDY~

THE SMELL OF fresh paint met me as I walked into the building that would be Lila's dance studio. It was a pale shade of blue, and the unpainted ceiling would soon look like the morning sky. She had told me about an artist she had coming in to paint it. There was still a lot to be done, but I was happy for her. She was so excited when she talked about her plans. I listened to her for over an hour last night. When she'd realized how long she'd been talking to me about it, she'd apologized. It had been cute.

Not one time in my life had someone made me forget Bliss. There was always an ache in my chest when I thought of her. Until now. That was gone. I knew why. Lila had become important to me. She had been so damn adorable that I couldn't think about anyone else. Bliss was what she should have always been to me now—a friend. A very good friend who I cared about but I could honestly say I was no longer in love with my best friend. I was happy Bliss had found Nate and that her life was full of joy.

I pulled my duffle bag up over my shoulder and headed across the large room toward the one door in the back. She had said to take that door and head straight up the stairs. Tonight she was cooking for the first time in her kitchen and she hadn't wanted to leave the food unattended, so she'd left the doors unlocked for me.

The paint smell disappeared when the heavy door closed behind me. I started up the stairs. I could smell garlic sautéing before I was halfway there.

"Eli?" Lila called out.

"Yep!" I replied.

I heard the tap of her feet as she walked in my direction. When I reached the top of the stairs she was there to greet me. She was breathtaking. Damn, it was good to be here.

"You're here!" she said grinning at me as if I wouldn't show up. Then she waved her hand out and spun around. "This is it. What do you think?"

The space was the ultimate bachelor pad. Lila had added a lot of soft yet colorful female touches to subdue its masculinity. However, the industrial look with the exposed beams had to have been designed with a man in mind. Nothing fancy. Just wide open and durable.

"I think I'd like to rent that room if Ophelia backs out," I said teasingly.

"It's great, isn't it? I love my view and the feel of the place."

I nodded. "Yes, it's great." So was my view. Lila had on a short white skirt with a sleeveless blue top that showed off her tan. Her hair was pulled up on her head in a messy knot. She wasn't wearing makeup, but she didn't need it.

"I don't have a bed in Ophelia's room yet but the sofa has a pullout bed, and it's a good one. I had checked before I bought it." I looked over at the living area; she had a tan leather sofa that was plush and wide. Two red and brown striped chairs and a large rectangular ottoman sat in the middle. The flat screen was massive, but then it could be seen from anywhere throughout the large flat.

"That looks comfortable enough to sleep on just like it is."

"It may be. But you're tall," she pointed out.

I'd try it out later. "Whatever you're cooking smells amazing. Can I help with anything?"

"Yes, you can slice the zucchini. I hate slicing vegetables," she said. "Put your duffle over by the sofa and come tell me about all the current happenings in Sea Breeze. I monopolized the conversation last night. I never heard what happened with Jude and Micah getting arrested."

I walked over to drop my bag by the couch as she walked back toward the kitchen.

"Damon, Micah's best friend, went and got them out before they called their dad. Micah may be twenty-five, but Jude is barely twenty. His dad would have been furious. They're both dumbasses for doing anything with Saffron. She's always looking for trouble."

"Saffron had invited them to go swimming at a friend's house she was supposedly house sitting for. There were topless girls there. They were a few of Saffron's stripper friends, although Saffron herself wasn't a stripper. Micah and Jude showed up, and the party had underage drinking. It got loud. The cops came. Micah told Saffron to hide because her father was a crazy ass son of a bitch who would lose his shit."

Eli continued. "Saffron hadn't been house sitting. They'd all been there without the owner's knowledge. It had been one of the stripper's ex-boyfriend's house. The ex-boyfriend and his wife were on vacation."

"Is the owner of the house going to press charges?" Lila asked as she handed me the zucchini.

"No. The stripper he had an affair with threatened to out him to his wife."

Lila laughed then. "Wow. Okay, that sounds like a movie.

Sea Breeze is more lively than Rosemary Beach. We rarely have drama. Nothing that interesting."

"That's because you don't have a Saffron Corbin."

Lila brushed by me twice to get something from the spice rack. I was trying not to assume she was doing it on purpose, but when she moved in close the third time I decided that was an invitation. I sat the knife down and grabbed her waist to pull her against me.

"I hope this is okay," I said in a whisper before claiming her mouth with my own. She was frozen at first, and then slowly melted against me, her arms going up around my neck. This was better than I remembered.

I heard the olive oil in the pan behind us sizzling. I knew I had to let her go, but the feel of her in my arms was so damn right it was hard. When she pulled back, she gave me a shy smile. "The onions will burn."

I let her go reluctantly, and she hurried over to move them around with a spatula. "You ready for the zucchini?" I asked still a little high from that kiss.

She glanced back at me over her shoulder and nodded.

I used that as an excuse to get near her. I took the vegetables then stood so close to her back that our bodies were touching. I bent my head and whispered in her ear. "I'll put them in there. You stir."

Lila shivered and then nodded. Pleased that I was affecting her this way, I began slowly pouring the sliced zucchini into the skillet. She was breathing rapidly, and I could see her pulse jumping in the curve of her neck. I pressed a kiss there unable to help myself.

A sharp intake of breath then she shivered again.

I reached over and turned the burner off then grabbed her and picked her up to set her on the bar. Spreading her knees open, I stepped between them and pulled her flush up against me before taking her mouth again. I could stay like this all night.

Her legs wrapped around my waist and she grabbed my face and kissed me back with just as much passion as I felt. It was intoxicating. Every touch, scent, sound she made drove me crazy. My biggest regret was having slept with her drunk like a one-night stand. She was special. I wanted to remember how it felt to be inside her. To know what her face looked like when she cried out with an orgasm.

Her hands moved down to my chest, and she ran them over my abs. Feeling each one as she kissed me. Our tongues tangled together. Our breathing synced. I ran my hands up her thighs wanting to touch her and watch her squirm and beg. To have her scent on my fingers.

She opened her legs more and the short skirt she was wearing slid up her thighs until it was all bare. I could see the white satin and lace of her panties. The damp fabric was clinging to her, and like a caveman, I wanted to beat on my chest that I had done that. I'd made her wet with just a kiss.

Running a finger over the thin, delicate fabric, I watched her face as her eyes flared and her cheeks became flushed. Slipping a finger inside, I groaned from pleasure at the heat that touched my finger. I could smell her arousal. She wanted me to touch her. She wanted this too.

"I kissed you here," the memory came back just that clearly. The smell hit me and with it came the memory of her legs thrown over my shoulders as I feasted on her like a fucking buffet I couldn't get enough of.

She nodded.

"You came on my tongue," my voice had gone husky with need.

"Yes," she whispered.

I started to lower to my knees, and she grabbed my arms.

"No. Don't."

I stopped and looked at her. I waited for a reason not to. I'd never had a female ask me not to taste her there.

She took a deep breath. "I'm not ready. I need time."

She wasn't drunk. We weren't at a bar. And I was acting like a sex-crazed maniac.

"I'm sorry. I got carried away. The memory . . ." I trailed off.

"It was amazing. But . . . I've been through other things since then. I need time. I like you, Eli. You make me smile. I don't want to mess this up. My head and heart need to be in the same place."

This wasn't just about taking our time. It was about Cruz Kerrington. I had his memory to compete with. But I wasn't afraid of that. He had hurt her. I never would. I could help her heal, and I was patient. God, was I so fucking patient. Lila fit me. We complemented each other. We had the same ideas, likes, beliefs, and we would make an excellent couple. I'd never let her down.

But she had to get over Cruz first and move on from what she went through. If I was going to give my heart to another woman I needed to know she wanted it. I could be patient and wait.

I let my hands rest on her thighs. "Okay. I can wait."

She sighed in relief and hugged me. "Thank you. I'm so lucky to have you. Right now, I would be lost and alone. But you're here and I . . . I'm really happy you are."

Chapter Thirty-One

♥ LILA KATE ♥

AFTER DINNER, I took Eli on a walk through town. He'd heard a lot about this place from Bliss, and he wanted to see more of it. The evenings here were very family friendly. Kids riding bikes along the sidewalks, couples walking by with ice cream cones to enjoy after a hot day, laughter from teens as they walked in groups, and most of them still wearing their swimsuits. It was the tourists, and it was what kept the area thriving.

"It's a vacation spot for the wealthy," Eli said with an amused tone. "This isn't like Sea Breeze. No condos just upscale coastal houses to rent. It draws a much different crowd. No drunk teens driving by yelling at each other through their sunroofs or rolled down windows. I like it."

"There are condos . . . just not like your condos. These are small and in two story buildings. Like that one there," I pointed to what I was talking about.

Eli laughed. "That's not condos. You've seen the twenty story buildings in Sea Breeze I'm talking about."

I agreed it was very different, and he wasn't even on the elite side of Rosemary Beach. That was secluded from the tourist. Kerrington Club was the beginning of the private area. I didn't want to take him there. Not yet.

"Lila Kate!" I heard my name and paused to glance around. Then I saw the red Mustang that Jace Montgomery had gotten for his high school graduation this year. I waved at him.

"Wrong side of town, babe. You lost?" I ignored the fact an eighteen-year-old called me "babe" simply because that was just Jace. He was kidding. He was always happy, and I'd known him since his birth. I'd gone to the hospital with my parents when he was born.

"I moved here," I told him as he pulled his car to a stop beside us.

"You moved to the town center?" he asked incredulously.

I nodded. "Yep. Jace this is my friend, Eli Hardy. Eli, this is Jace Montgomery."

Jace shot him a brilliant white smile. "Nice to meet you, Eli."

"Same here," Eli replied.

Then Jace looked back at me. "You're seriously living here?"

"Yes, Jace. Above the building where I will open my dance studio."

Jace's eyes went wide. "Damn that's awesome. Last I heard, you'd skipped town and Cruz had gone after you. At least that was what Blaze said."

"I'm back. Decided to start my life here."

He nodded. "Sorry about your grandmother. I wasn't in town when it happened. That's why I didn't come with my folks."

"Thanks. That's okay."

He smiled over at Eli again. "Keep this wild one straight. Y'all have a good night. I'll leave you to it."

"Bye, Jace," I said. He spun his wheels in response and headed back to the other side of town.

"He's eighteen. That's the only excuse I have for him," I told Eli when he was gone.

Eli laughed. "I figured that out pretty easily. I was eighteen once too."

The evening air was still warm, but I felt a shiver despite that. Pausing my heart did a funny little flutter, and I recognized it. Most of my life it had been reacting that way when Cruz was near. I wanted to pretend that I didn't feel it now. That it was gone. But I glanced over my shoulder because I needed to know if my body was still betraying me.

Sure enough, there he stood. His motorcycle parked outside my place. His arms crossed over his chest and his gaze locked on our backs as we walked away. He'd come to see me. The squeeze in my chest I felt because he was here to see me angered me. I wanted not to care. I wanted to be the strong independent woman who had moved on from him.

But I wasn't. I wanted to talk to him. I wanted to find out why he was there. Look at him and wish he was more. To wish he was the guy in a fairytale. To wish all kinds of pointless things that I'd never have. That would never be.

I didn't though. I turned my attention back to Eli, where we were walking, the night sky, anything but Cruz. It wasn't fair to leave Eli to talk to Cruz nor was I taking him back there with me. Cruz saw us. He knew Eli was here now. He also would know I chose Eli.

Each step we took further away from Cruz my heart ached. It was all I could do to not turn and run to him. To beg him to be different.

When Eli asked if I wanted an ice cream, I smiled up at him and said I did. Then I chanced a glance back. Cruz was still there.

He needed to leave. I needed him to go somewhere else now.

The Sugar Shack had a line out the door. It was the only ice cream place in town and it drew a crowd. We got in line and watched as kids begged for candy and other treats. Parents were on vacation and all smiles. The daily stress of the day gone. Many had a frozen adult beverage in their hands. I tried to focus on the scene around me and not look back.

"This place seems popular," Eli said.

"It's the only place for ice cream in town."

He looked surprised. "Someone needs to give them some competition."

I laughed at that, but took my chance to glance back at Cruz again.

This time he was gone.

The heaviness in my chest was there. My appetite for ice cream turned nonexistent. But I smiled anyway. I let myself be a part of the happiness around me. The sun kissed skin of the kids who had no worries, no heartbreak. If only life were still that easy.

"Eli," I said as I looked up at him.

"Yes?"

"I think I'm a waste of your time."

He looked sad for a moment, and then he put his thumb under my chin and cupped my face with his fingers. "You'll never be a waste of anyone's time."

"What if you're wrong?"

He gave me a small smirk. "Then I will have had an amazing memory of a girl who I was lucky enough to know."

If only his words made me feel better.

Glancing back one more time, I looked for Cruz or any signs he would magically reappear.

I heard Eli sigh softly. "He's gone, Lila."

Chapter Thirty-Two

~ELI HARDY~

EVERYTHING SEEMED BRIGHTER when you woke up to the smell of bacon. Last night hadn't been what I had hoped it would be. Lila was hung up on Cruz Kerrington, and I did my best to ignore the fact she wasn't completely with me last night. Her thoughts were somewhere else.

But I liked bacon. Stretching, I yawned and sat up to see Lila in a pair of pink pajamas and her hair in a ponytail standing in the kitchen cooking. That was a view I could spend the rest of my life enjoying. However, the more time I spent with her, the more I realized she was going to be the one that got away. The girl I talked about years and years from now when reminiscing about old times.

"Smells good," I said my voice still thick from sleep.

She lifted her head from whatever she was stirring in a bowl and grinned. "Nothing special. Pancakes and bacon. But I do have fresh blueberries and blueberry syrup to put on them. Even some whip cream if you're feeling adventurous."

I chuckled and stood up. "I'm always feeling adventurous.

Especially with pancakes."

Lila's gaze traveled down my bare chest, so I took my time reaching for the shirt I'd discarded last night. Let her take her fill. I knew my chest was impressive. I worked hard to keep my body in shape. I watched her, and when she realized she'd been caught checking me out she looked away and blushed adorably. I considered staying shirtless but decided that was desperate.

Tugging my shirt over my head, I walked over to the kitchen area and pulled out a stool across from where she was working. "I'd offer to help but you seem to have it under control and it looks like you're almost finished."

"I am. Want some coffee?"

I preferred tea, but I nodded. "Yeah, I'll get it though."

She turned and grabbed a cup. "I got it. Stay seated."

I watched her fix my cup. "Cream or sugar?"

"No thanks."

She handed it to me. "There you go."

I started to say more when banging on the door downstairs made us both pause. Lila frowned and we waited then. Soon after, it happened again. She moved the skillet off the eye of the stove. "I think someone is at the door."

"I'll check," I said standing up. "You're in the middle of all that."

"Okay thank you," she replied and went back to finishing the bacon.

I was almost down the stairs when I realized who I was about to greet at the door. It was a gut thing. I should have expected him to return after last night. Lila had been so busy looking back at Cruz that she hadn't realized I checked to see what had her attention. The guy stayed there awhile. Her not going to him was a bold move but I still thought she was weak. Him coming here this morning wasn't good.

But this wasn't my decision to make.

When I crossed the studio and got to the double doors of the entrance, there he was. Exactly who I expected. Looking like he'd drank a fifth of whiskey and hadn't slept a wink.

I wanted to leave his ass out there. Safely away from Lila. From hurting her even more. But then she could have a reason to be mad at me. I wasn't here to protect her. At least not from this.

"Cruz," I said as I opened the door.

He pushed by me and headed for the back door that led to the apartment. I'd been right about the whiskey—he reeked of it. This wasn't what she needed. He didn't seem to give a shit though.

"Are you trying to crush her?" I asked still standing at the door wishing he'd walk back out of it. He stopped and waited a beat before glaring back at me.

"You don't know shit. She doesn't love you. You're the fucking bandage." The hate in his tone was a bit alarming.

I shrugged. I wasn't affected by his hate and I wasn't scared of him. He was built. Tall. But he was hung over, and I had the upper hand. "I know she's hurting. She's trying to heal. But you won't let her. You keep ripping her open again and again."

He stared at me. Like he would like to murder me with his bare hands. I didn't move. I didn't want to fight the guy. Lila wouldn't be happy about it.

"I'm not good enough for her. Why can't she see that?" He sounded pained. Less anger more regret.

"I think she can. But can you?"

His hate flared back to life. "I love her. I would die for her. Take a fucking bullet for her. Can you say that? You barely know her. I've known her all my life. Loved her most of it. I just didn't want to." As he said the words, I could see the shock in his eyes. He surprised himself. I doubted he'd ever admitted that out loud.

"You have a funny way of showing love," I told him.

He ran his hands through his hair and the wild look in his eyes was a man that was wrecked. "She's destroyed me. I am fucking ruined. I need her. I'm so damn addicted to her I can't function. I can't stand her being with you. That you or someone like you will be the right one. Good enough. That she'll belong to another man. I can't fucking stand it!" he ended that with a roar and pulled at his hair like a man possessed.

"You've had too much to drink. Go home. Sleep it off. Think this through and if you still want to come back."

He shook his head. "I can't leave. Not with you up there with her."

This was worse than I thought. She was in love with a psycho. Why was no one in her life concerned about this? The guy needed some mental help.

"If you love her then be the man she deserves. This," I said waving my hand at him. "Is not that man. You're a fucking mess."

He glared at me and started toward me. His fists were clenched at his sides, so I prepare to defend myself. I hated to hit a drunk man, but I wasn't going to let him kick my ass either.

"Cruz!" Lila's voice stopped him. I looked over his shoulder to see her standing there. So innocent and sweet. This madman she was in love with didn't match up well at all.

He paused then turned to her. "Lila."

The tears in her eyes weren't falling yet, but they were there. Unshed.

"What are you doing?" she asked sounding like a teacher put out with an unruly student.

"I love you," he said.

Her tears broke free then. "I heard."

They stood there staring at each other. I walked around them and back upstairs to get my things. I didn't belong here. Not now.

Chapter Thirty-Three
~CRUZ KERRINGTON~

FIGHTING THIS WAS impossible. I'd tried. I had tried so damn hard. But I couldn't. Was I good enough for Lila Kate? No. Did she know all my dark secrets? No. Would she love me if she knew? Probably not. She'd hate me. I didn't want her to hate me.

She turned and grabbed Eli's arm as he came back downstairs with his bag. His staying the night here had been the last straw. I'd cracked. My chest exploding would have hurt less than seeing her with him last night. Eating fucking ice cream, walking around town like a couple. I couldn't stomach it. I knew after that I had to do something.

"Just let me talk to him. You don't have to go," she said to Eli.

"Yeah, he does," I argued.

She frowned at me. "No, he doesn't."

"Yes, I do," he said saving me from having to argue with her. Because his ass needed to go back to fucking Alabama and stay there. "This," he said pointing between Lila Kate and me. "This needs resolving. I'm in the way, and honestly, I don't want to watch any more of the train wreck."

I took a step toward him my hands balling into fists. Lila Kate was in front of me before I could take two steps. Both her hands on my chest. "Cruz. Don't. Just go upstairs. Please."

Her big beautiful eyes were telling me to go upstairs . . . to her apartment. That meant I wasn't the one leaving. So I backed away and nodded.

"Thank you," she whispered as if he couldn't hear her.

"Don't touch her," I warned him making sure he understood I'd find his ass. I'd track him down and make sure neither of his hands worked again.

"Cruz, please," Lila Kate begged.

I turned and walked to the back door only glancing back once.

"I'm sorry about all this," she told him. "I never expected him to come here."

"But you're glad he did," Eli replied.

"Yes," she said without hesitation.

I left them. She wanted me. She wasn't begging him to stay. Proclaiming she loved him. Crying over him. I hadn't lost her yet. It wasn't too late for us. I would worry about my secrets later. The shit I still had to end. Deal with. I'd handle it. For now, I just needed Lila Kate.

The smell of bacon filled the apartment when I reached the top stair. The large area was a great space. Open, roomy, and Lila Kate had put her touch on it. I smiled at all the reds and yellows. She loved bright colors. Somehow, she made colors that I normally wouldn't care for attractive.

There were pancakes on the bar along with blueberries and bacon. She had made him breakfast. Jealousy ate at me. The only thing keeping me sane was the fact the sofa bed was out and used. They hadn't slept together. The idea of them wrapped up together last night had been what sent me to drinking. At one point, I'd drunk enough that I'd passed out. Only slept three hours before I was awake again tortured over the idea of them together.

I picked up a piece of bacon and ate it, then went to see if there was milk in the fridge. I was hungry. I hadn't eaten all night, and the more I thought about Lila Kate cooking all this for Eli, the more I wanted to eat it. Take what he thought was his. It was mine first, dammit.

"I can't keep doing this with you, Cruz," Lila Kate said the moment she entered the apartment. She wasn't crying anymore. She was more intense. Serious. "This is messing with my head. I'm a wreck. That guy you just ran off is a good guy. He's sweet and kind. He likes me. He doesn't need women everywhere to fawn over him to make him feel like a man. He is perfect. Completely perfect. So why is it that the moment you show up I forget all that? Why can't you see that this is ruining me? This back and forth." Her hands were on her hips, and she was keeping her distance. I wanted her here with me. Eating this food. Smiling at me. Up on this bar with her legs spread while I fucked her. There was a lot I wanted from her. But only one thing was important.

"Do you love me?" I asked her. It was simple. It was what I needed to know.

She sighed and closed her eyes tightly. "Yes. You already know I do."

That was what I needed to hear. I walked around the bar and straight to her. She opened her eyes when she heard me approach. They were haunted with pain. Pain that I had caused. Pain that she didn't deserve. I'd make that up to her. I would spend my life doing it.

"Then forgive me. Please. Give me another chance. Because Lila Kate Carter, I'm completely in love with you. I can't see my life without you in it. All I want when I open my eyes every morning is to see you there beside me. And at night to sleep with you in my arms. Just, let me show you I can be that guy. The one you thought you had found in Eli. I can be him. Just a little more fucking exciting because he is too damn structured and you'd soon be bored as hell."

"Why now? What changed?" she asked. Still cautious and unsure.

"Because I can't fight this anymore. I thought I was protecting you from me, but I can be the guy you deserve. I love you so fucking much there will never be a man that loves you more. That much I can guarantee you."

She smiled. It was small and soft then she shook her head in disbelief. "I'm a fool."

That wasn't what I wanted to hear.

"No, you're not."

She tilted her head back. Her chin lifted. "Yes. I am. Because as I stand here and argue with you, I know that I am going to forgive you. I'll do it again too if I have to. Why can't I shake you, Cruz? Why? What is the insane hold you have on me?"

My heart felt so damn full I wanted to do a fist pump and let out a shout of victory. "I'm pretty damn sweet," I teased her.

She smirked. "No, you're not."

"Okay. fine. Maybe not sweet. But I can be. I'm going to be. I am going to be all you need me to be. I swear it."

"What happens when you get bored with me?"

I reached for her then. "I've known you all my life. Never once have you bored me. Not even when you were so uptight you could barely walk," I grinned as I said it.

She laughed. That had been what I was trying for. "That's not exactly smooth talking."

I held her back and pressed her up against me. "No? I'll work on that then."

Bending down I kissed her lips softly. She leaned into me and kissed back. A soft, pleased moan came from her mouth, and I tasted deeper. Held her closer. This was all I was going to need. It made all the other times, all the other girls and women pale. They were forgettable. Lila Kate had claimed my soul.

Chapter Thirty-Four

♥ LILA KATE ♥

THE LAST OF the blueberry pancakes I'd made for Eli were finished off by Cruz as he sat beside me at the bar. His left hand was on my thigh while he used his right hand to eat. He'd kept me close. Even after our kiss, he hadn't wanted to stop touching me. As if I were going to vanish.

As unreal as this all was, I was dealing with guilt over the way Eli had left. I'd tried to talk to him and convince him to stay but he'd been right. He and I never stood a chance as long as Cruz was taking up so much space in my heart.

"This was amazing. I was starving. A night full of regret and Jack Daniels will do that to you."

I smiled and started to move, but his hand clamped down on my leg. "Don't go."

"I was just going to clean up."

He turned to face me and captured my legs between his thighs. "It will keep. You don't have to clean it just yet."

The way he looked at me had me worried this was a dream and I was about to wake up. It was hard to accept. "You just want to sit here and look at each other then?" I asked him enjoying this. In case I did wake up soon and had to be heartbroken over it.

"We could," he said then his hands went to my pajama top and pulled it over my head. I hadn't put on a bra this morning since my pajamas were baggy. My breasts were bared to him. His focus on those and nothing else. "Or I could continue to get you naked, carry you over to that sofa bed and sink my dick into that silky hot pussy of yours," his voice had lowered to his sexy growl.

"Oh," I replied.

He chuckled. "Yeah, oh," he repeated and then I was in his arms and we were headed to the sofa bed.

He nibbled on my ear causing me to squirm in his arms and started whispering exactly what he wanted to do to me. Just like in New Orleans he was focused on me. How he could make me feel. But when he put me down I didn't lie back. I wasn't nervous. Not now.

I reached up and began to undo his jeans. He watched me. He didn't speak or move. I got them undone and pulled them down his hips until they fell to the ground and he stepped out of them. I then jerked his boxer briefs down and his larger than I remembered thick penis of his sprang free.

"You keep looking at my cock like that, and we aren't gonna have any foreplay," he warned.

I got on my knees and ran my hands up the front of his thighs. The muscles under my hands tensed. His body went completely still as if frozen. When my right hand wrapped around his hard shaft he groaned. I didn't give him time to react. My mouth covered the head, and I pulled as much into my mouth with one suck as possible.

"Fuuuuck," he groaned and his knees buckling. A hand was on my head, and his thighs were trembled. "Lila, Jesus."

As my mouth covered the smooth skin, my hand began to

easily slide up and down it with a pump after each lick and pull of my mouth. Cruz began panting. His breath was uneven and hard. I could hear it, and I savored the way he was completely under my control.

My tongue circled the head and he hissed as his hand fisted in my hair. My ponytail wrapped around his hand as he began to pull and push my head as I worked my mouth over him.

"I don't want to know why you're so good at this. Jesus, Lila, holy hell this is better than all the times I've imagined this while taking a shower."

I smiled up at him, and he smirked as his chest rose and fell rapidly. I watched him. Keeping our eyes connected as I ran my tongue over him. Teasing. Flicking the tip and then going back down on it.

"God, baby, just like that. Fuck, that's good."

I had never wanted to give a guy a blow job before. But Cruz. I'd imagined this and thought about it. Wished for it. More than once over the past few years.

"I can't," he groaned and pulled me back then tossed me on the bed. His eyes were dark, pupils dilated. With one tug, he had my pajama bottoms and panties off. The firm muscular body I was fascinated with covered me. "Open for me, Lila," he demanded.

My thighs fell open, and he captured both my wrists and held them over my head. Pinned to the mattress. "I was gonna be fucking sweet, but now I need this pussy. You've made me crazy, and this won't be anything resembling sweet, baby."

The first thrust was hard and I cried out from the pain but my body tingled with pleasure.

"You," he growled then plunged into me again. "Can't. Suck my dick like a pro and look like an angel and expect me to be sane."

I started to laugh when he filled me again and again, taking my breath. All my thoughts. Just the steady climb toward the release I knew was coming. The beautiful explosion that was only possible in his arms.

"I'm addicted to this. To you. Your goddamn pussy," he said it like he was angry about it. But then he began kissing my neck and taking little bites of my skin. It was erotic and sweet even if he thought it wasn't. Cruz would never be like Eli. He wasn't structured, polite, or predictable. Those were traits that I had. I craved something else. I craved the excitement of Cruz's wildness, dirty mouth, rule breaking. All the things I wasn't. It balanced me. He was my fit.

"Lila," he said as he lifted his head and sank into me completely.

"Yes," I was breathless.

"I love you, but I'm about to flip you over and fuck you like a paid for it."

I didn't have time to respond before he had me on all fours and his hands were on my hips as he began to pound into me from behind. I lost my breath. The angle where he entered me sent me closer to the climax I craved.

"So fucking proper and perfect with your ass up in the air for me to fuck," he said between thrusts. "Come for me baby," it sounded like a command. My body reacted like it was one.

I burst into flames and cried out his name. He pulled free and unloaded his release all over my backside. I felt the heat of the liquid as it hit me. We both went still. My body was humming from being taken so fiercely.

"I've got a thing for coming all over your body," he drawled.

"I like it," I admitted smiling into the pillow I had collapsed on.

"Stay right here," he said as if I had the energy to get up and go anywhere. I was close to passing out. Sleeping for a bit sounded good. My body spent in the best way imaginable.

A warm cloth startled me as it ran over my back, bottom and between my thighs. With one last wipe, he slid it over the sensitive area between my thighs and I gasped.

"Tender?" he asked.

I nodded.

He lay down beside me pulling me against him. "Sorry I was so rough. You set me off with the world class cock sucking."

I giggled and buried my head in his chest.

"Laugh all you want. You're a pro, and now that your mouth isn't on my dick I am a little worried about how you got so damn good."

I moved so I could see him. His arms still around me. "You've slept with hundreds of women, and you're worried about my blowjob abilities?"

He scowled. "Yes. I am."

I laughed then. Simply because I had only done this once before and I wasn't a big fan of it then.

"Glad you think I'm funny," he didn't sound pleased.

"What if I said I'm worried about the fact you can undress a girl and be inside her in less than thirty seconds?"

He was still scowling. "I'd say you knew I was a whore. I know you're a good girl. There's the difference."

I buried my head in his neck and traced a heart on his chest. "It was because it was you," I finally admitted.

"What?" he asked.

"It was you. I wanted to. I'd dreamed about it. Fantasized. You know."

He pulled back and tilted my head back until I had to look at him. "Are you telling me you've been fantasizing about sucking my dick?"

I nodded.

"Damn, baby. All you had to do was say 'Cruz, can I suck your dick?' and I'd have made that dream come true a lot faster."

Chapter Thirty-Five

~CRUZ KERRINGTON~

I HAD SHIT to fix. It was vital that I handled it before it was too late. Some secrets were best kept that way. Mine was one of them. I wasn't going to lose Lila Kate now that I had enough guts to admit I wanted her. That I loved her. I'd jumped in and done this. I wasn't letting go. Nor was I going to let her.

She'd become as important to me as breathing. Scary as hell. But the truth.

Leaving her to work at her studio while I went to the club for a meeting with Dad would have been the safe thing. The smart thing. But the idea of leaving her hadn't been appealing so I asked her to come with me, and we'd have lunch.

She didn't want this world. She had run from it. She had moved across town. Yet I was reminding her that I was this world. I would one day own the club and all that came with it. Sure, she knew where my future was but I still didn't want to remind her. Not this damn soon.

When we pulled up to valet and got out of the car to go inside, she seemed happy enough. I slid my arm around her waist and she didn't freeze or act nervous. She was fine with this public display of affection. I was just beginning to enjoy myself when Shelby, a waitress whose last name I did not remember, came walking out of the dining room. I muttered a curse under my breath when her eyes locked on me and she smiled. Completely nonplussed by the fact my arm was around Lila Kate's waist.

"Cruz," she said giving me a smile that was too familiar. Too damn sexual.

"Hello," I replied with a nod hoping to keep walking on past her. She was an employee; therefore, it was a given I should know who she was. It wasn't a given, however, that I should know that she got a Brazilian wax once a month.

"I'm just getting off the breakfast shift." She winked at me as if this meant something.

"Then enjoy the rest of your day." Hopefully, she took the hint. Her eyes shifted from me to Lila Kate, and they widened as if just now realizing I was with someone.

"Are y'all . . ." she didn't finish that question as she wagged her finger back and forth at both of us.

"Yes, we are," I replied. "Enjoy your Saturday." I then moved on hoping Shelby was done with her questioning.

"You don't have to get so tense when that happens. Cruz. I've known you my entire life. It's going to happen a lot."

I gazed down at Lila Kate. "I wish I could make it stop. I don't want you to be uncomfortable."

She smirked. "Dating you means dealing with all your past relationships."

"Shelby wasn't a relationship. She was a fuck."

Lila Kate sighed. "I was trying to be more delicate."

That made me laugh. "Shelby never considered me a relationship either. I promise."

With a small lift of her shoulder she said, "I don't imagine any girl did."

Never had I wished I could go back and change shit. Until now. Lila Kate's opinion of me wasn't great. And what sucked most was it wasn't even accurate. I was much worse than she thought.

"I'll get a table and order a drink while you meet with your dad," she told me as we neared the restaurant entrance.

"Okay. I won't be long. I'll let him know you're waiting on me. That should make his fucking year."

"Are you ready to tell your parents about this? Don't you think we should wait until you're sure?" The doubt in her voice and her words stung. Even now after the dramatic scene I'd made this morning, she was still being cautious. I deserved it.

I pulled her hand up to my chest and pressed a kiss to her fingers. "I'm not sure where I wasn't clear this morning. But I am positive. There is no question in my mind. Is there in yours?" Because if she still didn't know if she wanted to do this I might have to resort to drastic measures. Like kidnaping her and taking her off to a cabin in the mountains and making sure she was as addicted to me as I was her.

I sighed inwardly. The fact I'd just thought something like that meant I was sunk too deep.

"I've been sure since I was fourteen," she replied.

I had started pushing her away even back then. When I knew we had something, but I'd hurt her in the end. So I hurt her in the beginning. I had a lot of years to make up for now.

I grabbed the back of her head and kissed her until she was clinging to me and our chests were rising and falling rapidly. "I love you," I reminded her. Then I pressed one more kiss to her lips before turning toward my father's office.

I hadn't been this damn happy about being here, breathing air, and eating at this place in a long damn time. Since childhood at least.

I glanced back to make sure Lila Kate had gone into the dining room before knocking n my dad's door.

"Come in," he called out.

For once I wasn't dreading it. I opened the door, and Dad stood there leaning against the front of his desk with his arms crossed over his chest. A frown on his face and his eyes glaring in my direction.

"Explain to me what I just saw out there. Go slowly. Be thorough."

Shit.

"I'm not sure what you're referring to," was my lame response.

"Cruz, I'm not in the fucking mood."

This was going to have to be dealt with sooner or later. I figured sooner would at least be getting it out of the way. "I'm in love with Lila Kate."

Dad's glare faded, and his eyebrows drew together as he studied me. "In love? Like only one woman in love?"

Jesus, he had a low opinion of me. "Is there another love? Because I always believed that if you were in love, it was with only one woman. Unless you're in love with women in general."

"You're a smartass," he said scowling again. "When did you decide you were in love with Lila Kate?"

Why did this matter? I wasn't here to defend myself. I would have to do that with Grant. I shouldn't have to do it with my father. "Does it matter?"

I gave me one sharp nod and continued to glare at me.

"When I thought I was going to lose her. That's when."

"Lose her? When did you have her?"

"I didn't have her, but it was the idea that she could love someone else. Forget me. Move on. It was a slap in the face. One I needed."

Dad stood up straight and groaned. "That's not the answer I

wanted to hear. You can't just think you love her in order to keep her loving you. Then get bored and break her heart. That's cruel son. Selfish. I taught you better than this."

"I've loved her or a long time. Okay. I knew if I let myself I'd feel something special. But Lila Kate is . . . she's important. I couldn't hurt her. I was protecting her."

I watched as he rubbed his forehead as if frustrated. This wasn't his business. We weren't kids who were just caught fucking in the backseat. "You wanted to meet with me about the Kipling franchise," I reminded him.

"You're changing the subject."

I nodded. "Yep."

He started to say something else and stopped. "Fine. You are both adults. If you want to do this, I can't stop you. But Lila Kate isn't like the women you typically spend time with. She's fragile, sweet, unsure . . . I don't want you to hurt her."

I looked directly at my dad. "Nothing has ever been this serious in my life. I'll kill anyone who hurts her."

Dad sat there a moment then raised one of his eyebrows. "Well, son, I guess I lost that bet."

"What?"

He walked over to his side of the desk. "I told your mother you'd be a bachelor until you were at least forty. She bet me you'd fall in love before the year was over. She said she just had a feeling."

Annoyed at both my parents, I stood up. "I can't believe y'all were betting on that. I hope she just emptied your fucking pockets."

Dad chuckled. "I won't tell you what the wager was . . . you couldn't handle it."

Chapter Thirty-Six

♥ LILA KATE ♥

THE OOLONG TEA I'd ordered was getting cold as I waited on Cruz. I'd taken a few sips but my thoughts were elsewhere, and I'd forgotten about it while I pondered this situation. I hadn't been kidding when I had said that I would be dealing with a lot of "Shelbys." It was just the way things were.

The problem was I immediately started comparing myself to her and finding my faults. She was taller, leggy, her hair was blonde and curly. She was confident. I couldn't do this every time we came in contact with a female Cruz had slept with. That would eventually make me miserable. I had to build some confidence. I had to think about my good qualities and remember that Cruz had said he loved me.

I was almost positive he'd never said that to another woman. It wasn't a Cruz-type behavior to proclaim love.

"Sorry it took so long," Cruz's voice startled me, causing me to jump a little. He grinned, obviously amused. As he sat down, he added, "You were in deep thought."

I nodded. "Yeah. Just thinking."

That wiped out his smile. "About?"

He was as unsure as I was. That helped a little bit. I wasn't the only one feeling vulnerable. "About everything. Nothing specific."

He leaned forward and looked at me with a serious and intense expression. "Please don't question this or me. Give me time. I can be all those things you think I can't."

I slid my hand over the table and covered his. "I know. That's not what I was thinking about."

He seemed relieved and his thumb wrapped around my finger. "Good."

"Hello Lila Kate, Cruz," the interruption was from Kelsey Torrent, the head of marketing for the Kerrington Club.

Cruz's hand slipped away from mine abruptly, and he sat up straight in his chair. No one else would notice he'd done it so smoothly. But Kelsey's interruption had startled him. She'd been working for the club for five years now. I didn't know her that well.

"Hello, Kelsey," Cruz replied barely glancing up at her.

Kelsey smiled as if our greeting had been much warmer. I felt awkwardness that didn't make sense hanging over us. "Hello," I said trying to make up for Cruz's response.

Kelsey barely glanced at me. "Your father wants to see you," she said to Cruz. Her tone was annoyed. She didn't seem to care much for him. I wondered if she felt threatened by his position at the club. I could imagine she wasn't excited about answering to someone twenty years younger than her in the coming years.

"I just left his office," Cruz replied.

She was trying to cover her sudden anger. But I could see it behind her fake smile. "That may be so, but he wants you to come back. I'm sure," she glanced at me with a tight smile. "Miss Carter can finish lunch alone."

I started to tell him I could just head back to the studio and work, but Cruz spoke first. "I'll eat my lunch, and then see what

Dad needs in his office."

Kelsey Torrent wasn't pleased. She was more than annoyed. When she spun around and walked away, I let out a breath I'd been holding. I thought the two of them were going to cause a scene. Which would have probably gotten her fired, and Cruz in serious trouble.

"I don't think she likes you very much," I said quietly once she was out of the dining room.

He shrugged as if he didn't care, but he was tense. That had bothered him. I felt bad for him. Having to join a company like this and deal with employees who didn't like that he'd be their boss eventually. "She's uptight," was all he said.

We ordered our food and Cruz tried to relax unsuccessfully. I wished he'd just find out what his father wanted instead of worrying about ignoring him or putting him off. I glanced at my phone and decided to fib to Cruz to relieve him from this lunch with me. He would worry the entire time if he didn't answer to his father.

"Oh, that's the decorator I need to meet with. She's available now but won't be again until Thursday. I need to see what she can do and get a quote. Do you mind?"

"No, that's fine. You need to meet with her. I'll be there later today. I need to deal with my dad first."

"Thank you. I'm sorry. I can just ask the kitchen to pack up my food to go."

He stood then. "I'll get it from the kitchen. They'll take their time otherwise." He was being helpful, but his head was somewhere else. We were new. Our relationship and being seen in public was new. So, I didn't feel like I could question him too much about what was distracting him. I would have to let him tell me what was going on when he was ready.

I got my purse and drank the rest of my tea before he walked back with a bag containing my lunch. It was hard to miss the eyes that followed him as he walked through the restaurant. Many spoke to him. Others watched him like he was a meal they wanted. I couldn't blame them. He was so very easy to look at.

When he reached the table, I stood up, and he kissed me. Right there for everyone to see. It was like he was making a claim. Letting them all know. But in reality, he was showing me he was serious. I took the bag once the kiss ended and felt my cheeks turn warm.

"You're blushing," he smirked.

"Yes," I whispered. "These people may not all know me, but they all know you."

"They know you, Lila Kate Carter."

My cheeks were flaming now.

"God, you're cute," he said, grinning now. His earlier tension had eased. "I'll see you shortly."

With a nod and a shy smile, I left with my gaze straight ahead, afraid to make eye contact with anyone. Cruz had already disappeared in the other direction.

"Lila Kate," a female voice stopped me. I turned to see Adelle Boyd giving me a calculating look. She sat at a table with her mother and younger sister. They were all three in tennis skirts as if they'd just come inside from the courts. Which they probably had.

"Hello," I said to the table already knowing what this was about. That kiss was sweet, but I knew it would get me some attention I didn't want. Or I should say, drama.

"Are you dating Cruz?" she asked a touch of disbelief in her tone

I forced a smile. "Yes."

Her mother made a strange sound in the back of her throat. I didn't look at her.

"Since when?"

"It's new," I told her sweetly. What I wanted was to be rude and tell her it was none of her business though.

Her mouth turned up into an amused grin. "It'll also be short."

Both mother and sister made muffled laughs. I didn't have time for this.

"Y'all have a wonderful day too," I said before I walked off hoping no one else stopped me.

They didn't. Once outside I breathed a sigh of relief. That was just the beginning. I had to learn to handle people's reactions better.

Chapter Thirty-Seven
~CRUZ KERRINGTON~

I TURNED AND went the other direction as Lila Kate left the Club. My stomach clenched as my demons chased me. The reason I had kept my distance from Lila Kate, the reason I had wanted her and now knew I loved her but would never get close enough was breathing down my neck. I'd taken this chance and gone after her even though I had shit that could destroy us before it ever began. I had sworn to her I wouldn't hurt her. I was about to make sure I kept that promise.

Turning left instead of right, I headed for Kelsey's office. My father hadn't sent her for me. She'd seen me with Lila Kate, and she'd come after me. Normally, she didn't interfere with my sex life. She was a married woman after all. But she knew . . . Lila Kate Carter was different.

I didn't knock on her door. I just walked inside. She was standing on the other side of the room with a glass of ice water in her hand staring out the window.

"You can't date her," was all she said. She didn't even turn around.

"I can do whatever the fuck I want to do, Kelsey," I replied angry that she thought she had some magic pussy that could control me. Maybe that was true when I was sixteen and she'd brought me in this office one night late after a ball and sucked my dick for the first time. She'd had some power over me. But I wasn't a boy anymore. I'd had many women since she introduced me to sex.

"I don't care about all your whores. That's all they are. You're a man. Men like sex. They like variety. I'm okay with that. But not her. You know she's not a whore. You want more with her," she turned to me then. "Am I right?"

"Yes, you're correct. What we did wasn't right. You're married. We should have stopped a long time ago. Hell, we never should have started. But I was a horny teenage boy, and you took advantage of that. I didn't care about your husband then. I should have, but my sex drive was running the show. We are done. I love her. There is only her for me."

Kelsey was a beautiful woman. Tall, slender, generous breast size and a freak when it came to sex. I'd fucked her right on that desk many times in many different positions. And she'd watched me fuck other girls and had waiting to fuck me after because it turned her on. That had been fun. Before. But the past year, she'd gotten clingier. Needier. More possessive.

"Is that what you think? That you can fuck me for five years then just walk away. Just like that?"

"We never had a relationship. We fucked. It was never exclusive. You're married. Remember? I can do what the hell I want to do. This thing we did is over."

The blaze in her eyes was never good. She didn't like being told no. She typically got whatever she wanted. I was more than positive I wasn't the only teenage boy she'd fucked. She liked them young. She told me so when she bared her tits to me and sucked me off the first time.

While having sex with her the past five years had been fun and games, I knew it was wrong. It was something Lila Kate would never understand. I had to make sure it was buried. Forgotten.

"You think you have control over this?" Kelsey asked as she took a step toward me. She was unbuttoning her shirt. Once that would have gotten me excited. Right now, it just pissed me off.

"Yes, I do. It's done. Over," I was direct. Looked her in the eyes and made sure she saw how serious I was.

Her blouse was open, but I didn't look down. I didn't want that from her. Not anymore.

Her hand was on my dick, and she squeezed. "Really?" her voice had dropped to a purr.

"Yes, really," I replied, backing away from her. "Just stop. You're pathetic."

She froze and her previously smiling face returned to a state of fury. "You little spoiled bastard. You will regret this."

"No, I won't," I assured her as I turned and walked away. The end of what I'd been doing with Kelsey was way overdue. When I was almost out the door, she found a way to stop me.

"I'm pregnant. My husband is sterile. I was preparing to tell him about us. I still am. You can't walk away from this, Cruz. You're going to be a daddy."

I glared at her. Even now she was lying. "I've never fucked you without protection. Ever. So it's someone else's baby. Not mine. You tell him it's mine and you'll have to prove it." I wasn't a teenage boy anymore. She couldn't trick me into shit.

Her eyes teared up. "Condoms aren't one hundred percent effective."

"Birth control is," I shot back.

She wiped a single tear as it rolled down her cheek. "I stopped taking them a year ago. I want a baby. I want your baby."

I shook my head. No. She was lying. This was her way to

manipulate. It wasn't going to work. "You are a liar," I roared not caring who heard me then stormed out of the office. Away from the club and the dark shit that was now catching up with me. I thought she'd keep quiet for fear of losing her marriage. She had told me once she loved her husband, but he didn't take care of her sexually. She needed more. The dirtiness, the excitement. I had felt sorry for her and didn't understood how a man wouldn't enjoy her insane sexual needs. It had been fun. Now I saw the fun was fucked up.

It was also going to destroy me if she went through with this lie. I had to find a way to stop this. To protect Lila Kate. I never wanted her to see that side of my life. To know the sordid shit I'd done.

Getting to Lila Kate was all I needed right now. To hold her. Smell her. Feel her. The brightness in her world made my damaged past fade away.

The drive to her studio was only a few miles, but it felt like an eternity. The fear she'd know and hate me weighed on me. Her refusal to listen to me and to love me was clawing at my heels. I drove faster and focused on getting to her.

I took long fast strides from my car to her door. When I jerked it open, there Lila was. She'd already changed into paint-stained clothing, threw her hair in a bun and was dancing to music as she cleaned out a paint brush. She was good. Perfect. Pure.

I locked the door behind me and went to her. She glanced up, startled at first and then she smiled.

"Hey," was the only thing she had time to say before I was there in front of her. I backed her up until she was behind the corner blocking us from the windows. The shadows there didn't mask the surprise and excitement on her face.

I didn't take time to kiss and hold her. I couldn't. The wolves that were chasing me, haunting me, had me desperate. I jerked down her shorts and panties then quickly shoved my jeans down until my dick was free. Grabbing her by the waist I picked her up, pressed her between the wall and my body then thrust into her with a groan.

She grabbed my shoulders and cried out my name. That only caused this wild intense pounding in my head to get worse. My mouth devoured hers tasting and taking it all. I was fucking her while loving her.

"This is mine," I told her biting at her neck. "You can't leave me." My words would sound crazy to her, but they came out anyway.

"Okay," she said as her head was thrown back against the wall and her throat exposed to me while I licked and left my mark on it.

"I will always need this. Need you. I'm addicted to you. Fucking addicted."

She moaned and I pounded harder. Wanting to get so damn deep that we were like one person. No one else would ever be this for me. She would be all I needed. Being inside her made the darkness and the lies go away. All that mattered was her. This. Us.

"Oh God," she cried then bit my shoulder. She was trembling in my arms. "AH!" Her orgasm squeezed my cock and I let go with her.

"Fuck! That's it, baby. Come all over my dick."

"Ahhhh! Cruz! I can't," she was clinging to me now. Her arms wrapped around me. Her head in the crook of my neck.

I exploded inside her jerking free a little too late.

"Shit," I groaned as the rest of my release coated the inside of her thigh.

We stood there in the corner sweaty, wrapped together, panting. This was what I'd never done with anyone. I'd always been careful. But my insanity when it came to Lila Kate had taken over and it had been the last thing on my mind.

"It's okay," she finally whispered. "Remember I'm on the pill."

I nodded and kept holding her. Wishing I was still inside. Pulsing my release until it ran freely out of her. Making her mine.

I was scaring myself.

Chapter Thirty-Eight

♥ LILA KATE ♥

I HAD INTENDED to get a lot done this weekend. But Cruz had changed that plan. After the wild sex we'd had downstairs, he'd taken me to the shower where he was now bathing me slowly. He wasn't talking much. The haunted look in his eyes like he was running from something and needed me to protect him was hard to miss. It was as if he was safe as long as we were touching.

He was more important than the studio. All that could wait. For now, I enjoyed him. Being with him. He needed reassurance. This was new. I would say I needed reassurance too, but the way he was hovering over me I was getting plenty.

Sunday we slept in, ate breakfast that we cooked together and watched movies all day.

When Monday morning came, so did Ophelia. I had just gotten out of the shower and was looking forward to the coffee I smelled in the kitchen when I heard her say "Holy shit. This is not happening."

I grabbed a towel, wrapped it around me and hurried in there. Ophelia was standing in the kitchen with a suitcase staring open mouthed at Cruz who was wearing nothing but boxers while he held a tin of muffins I had left in the oven.

"Morning, Ophelia. Can't say I'm happy you're back," Cruz said as he turned to look at me and winked.

Ophelia swung her gaze toward me. "Ohmygod," was all she could get out. Her eyes were wide, and she dropped the bag on her left shoulder to the floor with a loud thump. "What happened?"

"It's rude to ask for details, O. You should know better," Cruz was taunting her.

She glared at him. "I don't want details! I want to know that there is an explanation that doesn't include the two of you," she wagged a finger between us and said, "doing it."

Cruz laughed loudly. "Did you just say 'doing it?'" he asked then laughed some more.

She gave up on him and turned completely to me. I was still standing there silently unprepared. "Lila Kate?" she prompted.

"I, well, uh," I glanced at Cruz who was eating a muffin and grinning enjoying this a little too much. "Yes, we did it," I blurted out.

Cruz began to laugh some more.

"Have you lost your mind?" she asked pointing back at him. "He's a whore!"

"Hey, I've got feelings. You're crushing them," he didn't sound crushed at all.

She rolled her eyes and shook her head.

"No, I'm, uh, we are, you see," I was fumbling.

"We're exclusive. I've given up my man whore ways because Lila Kate gave me a taste and I got addicted. There's also the small very important detail that I am in love with her."

His explanation wasn't as sweet and romantic as the things he'd said to me, but my chest swelled anyway. That was as sweet as Cruz let the world see him. He'd been open and just made himself vulnerable by admitting that.

"In love?" Ophelia repeated it like it was a foreign word she'd never heard before. She looked back at me.

"Yes. I love him, too."

Defeated, she sat down on her suitcase and shook her head. "I need a moment. This . . . just wow."

"Muffin?" Cruz asked holding the pan out to her and then me. "They're fucking delicious. Grab one now because I'm gonna eat them all."

I walked past Ophelia, and she watched me like I was about to grow wings and fly off. As she sat down at the bar, I took the muffin pan and picked a muffin out, then went to pour myself some coffee.

"Are you going to," she waved at Cruz. "Walk around in your underwear a lot?"

He smirked. "No. You're not that lucky. I wasn't aware you'd be barging in so early."

"It's ten," she replied.

"Exactly—the crack of dawn."

"Lila Kate, you can't be serious about this. He's . . . he's Cruz!"

I smiled into my coffee cup. This was our first encounter with a friend or family member. I imagined this was going to happen a lot.

"What about Eli? I thought you liked him."

Cruz's smile vanished, and he scowled. "She doesn't," he replied. His teasing tone now gone.

I put my cup down. "Eli is a great guy. But I've been in love with Cruz a long time."

"Why?"

Cruz laughed again. "Damn, Ophelia. I didn't know your opinion of me was so high."

She cocked her head and stared at him with a "get real"

expression. "You have screwed most of my friends. And when I say most, that includes all of them. And now you're sleeping with Lila Kate."

He winced. "Could we not discuss my past? That's behind me. I'd like to leave it there."

Ophelia stood up and let out a heavy sigh. "This is going to end badly. Then Grant Carter will murder you. Mark my words," she said as she carried her suitcase and bag to the bedroom that was to be hers.

I slipped an arm around Cruz's waist and leaned into him. "She'll be more positive soon."

He kissed the top of my head. "That's what I expect we will get from everyone in our life."

He was probably right. So I just kept my mouth shut and hugged him to me. "I'm happy. I've never been happier," I assure him.

"Me too. And honestly that scares the hell out of me."

"Why?" I asked tilting my head back to look up at him.

"Because I know what this feels like and I can't live without it or you."

"You'll never have to so that's not a problem. I'm not going anywhere."

That desperate, haunted look shadowed his eyes again. I wished I could soothe him and his concerns. I was the one who should be worried. Not him.

"Can y'all put on clothes at least while I get one of the boxes out of my car?" Ophelia reminded us of her presence.

Cruz jerked the towel around me off and I scrambled to get it from him. "You are taking all the fun away," he told Ophelia. "I like her in a towel. Easier to get her naked."

"God! You are a pig," she replied and went back down the stairs.

I slapped at his chest and grabbed the towel from him. "Stop that!"

He pulled me to his chest. "Think she'd care if we went up to your room and went another round?"

As tempting as that was, I wasn't doing that to Ophelia. "Get dressed Cruz," I told him, then grinned and left my towel off as I walked up the stairs to my room.

"Damn, you are asking for it," he threatened.

I glanced back and winked at him. "Save it for later."

"I take it back," he said staring up at me.

"What?"

"You're not a china doll, and nothing about you is cold."

I smiled and bit my lip to keep from grinning too big.

"You are incredibly tough, and that body is so fucking hot I won't ever get enough."

They weren't words you'd ever hear in a sonnet but coming from Cruz Kerrington it was poetry.

Chapter Thirty-Nine
~CRUZ KERRINGTON~

OPHELIA MOVING IN with Lila Kate wasn't ideal, but over the next week we made it work. I even started getting along with my dad better, but that was mostly due to my showing up on time to work. Being at the meetings he required and all the other shit I had been ignoring.

Thinking about August when I had to go back to school sucked. Lila Kate was finished. She'd be here, and I would leave. I didn't like it. Worrying about it right now just gave me more to stress over. Avoiding Kelsey had been my biggest hurdle at work. She hadn't said anything to my dad, or I would know. I was hoping that she had been bluffing to scare me.

Regardless, the kid wasn't mine. I was willing to do a paternity test to prove it. That was if there even was a baby. I doubted that too. When I was sixteen, she'd been the sexy, exciting older woman. However, over the past year I had started noticing the crazy boiling under the surface.

The summer crowd was already up and in full swing when I walked out of Lila Kate's studio at eight in the morning. I had planned on walking to the coffee shop across the parking lot and getting Lila Kate one of those fancy teas she liked and a muffin. I definitely hadn't been expecting Grant Carter to be standing against his truck with his arms crossed over his chest glaring at me like he wanted to take the life from my body with his bare hands.

Shit.

"Grant," I said trying to not look guilty of staying the night with his daughter

"Not here for bullshit, boy."

I didn't assume he was. "No, sir. Don't imagine you are."

He dropped his hands to his sides and looked up at the windows to Lila Kate's loft. "That girl in there is the other half of my world. She and her momma have been every dream, every wish, every damn thing that means anything to me from the moment I held her in my arms."

"I understand that," I began and he took a step toward me his scowl deepening. "No. you don't. You don't understand a goddamn thing boy. You've never had a woman you loved more than life itself nor have you held a precious baby girl in your arms that is a miracle and knew that your life would be to protect her. You do not know what that is."

He was right there. I nodded afraid if I said anything until he was ready for me to he'd break one of the bones in my face. I liked my face the way it was.

"She is just like her mother. Kind, sweet, smart, and when she loves, she loves with everything she has. That's a lot for a man to handle. A lot for him to cherish. I didn't realize it with her momma right away and nearly lost the only thing I had worth living for. Her dad wanted me dead. I don't blame him."

I nodded, still not speaking.

Grant got in my face his shoulders wider and his arms thicker than my own. "If you fuck with my baby girl's heart I won't give one rat's ass who your parents are. All I've seen you do is fuck around. Play games. Enjoy women. But that girl up there," he said pointing for emphasis. "She's not the kind you do that with. Because I will tell you right now," he then pointed his finger in my face. "She has to love you, or you wouldn't be here. She would have never climbed on your bike and rode off like she did. That was not Lila Kate. She was acting on feelings for you. So either you have the same feelings for her, or you make a clean break and get the hell out of town before I can find you. Do I make myself clear?"

This was my turn to speak. "Yes sir," I said. "I know all those things about her. It's why I kept my distance for so long. But when she left, I knew I was going to lose her or any chance with her. I had to make a decision and I went after her. I told myself it was to protect her, but I knew deep down what I was doing. I love Lila Kate. I don't need anyone else."

Grant's scowl eased some but he still didn't look convinced. "I like you. I like your family. But I can't just trust anyone with my baby girl. Don't know if I ever will. I won't stop watching. I won't back off. You hurt her, expect me to come after you."

Jesus. It was a wonder Lila Kate had ever had a date in high school. I was expecting him to get his gun out of the truck and start waving it around any minute. "I will never hurt her."

He didn't look like he believed that. "Your past ain't pretty boy. It could come back to haunt you. If it were up to me, she'd leave you alone. Find a guy who didn't make it his goal to fuck the entire female population in this town. But it's not up to me. She's a woman. It's her choice. But I'm her daddy, and if you fuck this up there will be no place safe for you. I'll find you."

"Daddy!" Lila Kate's voice called out, and I glanced over my shoulder to see her standing at the front door in her pink fluffy heart robe with a very unhappy frown on her face. Luckily, it was directed at her father. Not me.

"Hey, baby," he replied.

She took long strides toward us. "This had better not be what I think it is," she said.

He shrugged like it was no big deal. "I'm your father. I was just coming to visit and found Cruz leaving your apartment. Making sure he was clear on some things."

Like the fact he was going to murder me if I hurt his daughter. I didn't mention that though.

"I don't need you to threaten the men in my life daddy," she told him.

"Men?" Grant and I both said in unison. There were no other men.

She rolled her eyes at both of us. "Oh, good grief. The 'man' in my life. I am an adult. I can have whoever I want sleep over. I can date whoever I want. And I can love whoever I want. You have to trust me to take care of myself."

"I do," he said giving her a charming smile that I sure as hell hadn't been given. "Just making sure Cruz was on the same page as you. That's all."

Lila Kate put her hands on her hips. "And what page is that?"

"That he was as serious about this as you are."

"And that is what I am saying. It isn't your business."

"You're my daughter, and that will never change. I'll make shit my business when it comes to protecting you for as long as I am alive."

Lila Kate sighed and gave me an apologetic look. "Are you having a change of heart now?" she asked me.

I smirked. As if Grant Carter could make me stop wanting her. "No. Not even close."

Her eyes went soft, and for a moment I forgot her father was even out there with us ruining a perfectly good morning. Our quiet breakfast was not going as planned.

"Jesus," Grant muttered. Then he walked over and hugged Lila Kate. "I can't help it you know," he whispered.

"I love him," she said her gaze shifting to me.

"And that makes him the luckiest man other than myself that I know."

Lila Kate grinned up at her father then.

I had been expecting this. I was glad it was over. Now I just had to make sure the Kelsey shit was done. That was one time bomb that threatened everything. If I lost Lila Kate over her, I would gladly let Grant put me out of my misery.

Chapter Forty

♥ LILA KATE ♥

MOM HAD CALLED me to meet her for lunch at the
club today. I'd been so busy I hadn't seen much of her.
Between getting the studio ready and spending time
with Cruz, my days were packed. I was just about to walk inside
the main building at the club when my phone vibrated. When I
checked, it was a text from Eli.

He was good about checking on me once a week if not more.
Cruz wasn't crazy about our friendship, but he allowed it. If he
knew I'd had drunken sex with Eli, I doubted he'd be okay with
it. That was before us so I figured it wasn't important to discuss.

I didn't ask about all the girls he'd slept with before me.

Studio almost ready? Eli's text asked.

I stopped walking and replied. *Another two weeks and it will be
open for business. About to have lunch with my mom. Text back later.*
I dropped my phone back into my purse and looked up to see
Kelsey standing a few feet in front of me.

Her eyes were red and swollen from crying. It was so unlike
her. She was always so businesslike, I couldn't imagine her as

emotional. Her gaze was locked on me. Almost as if I were the source of her pain. I glanced around me to see if there was anyone else around but it was just me.

"I need to speak with you," she said her voice hoarse with emotion.

She was upset so it wasn't like I could say, "No thanks. I have a lunch date with my mom."

Instead, I just nodded.

"Can you come in my office?" she asked.

I nodded again, and she turned and headed in that direction. I glanced around one more time. I didn't want to go to this woman's office but I also didn't see a way out of accepting her request unless I was rude.

The door was open as she walked inside. Reluctantly, I followed.

She stood at the door and closed it after I entered. I wished she'd left it open. Something about her made me nervous.

"I'll be brief. There is just something you need to know. I tried handing it with Cruz but he isn't cooperating. He's," she paused and teared up again. "I'm sure you know how cruel and selfish he can be."

That got my attention. "Cruz isn't either of those things," I said in defense of him. This woman's issues with his position at the club needed to be dealt with by Woods.

Her tear-stained face looked less defeated and more like the haughty woman I'd seen when she had spoken to Cruz last week when we had been eating.

"You're so young and naïve," she said with a disgusted look in her eyes. "You aren't in a fairy tale. Cruz isn't your prince charming, and he's not the kind of guy that will settle down and marry you. He needs sex with different women. A variety," she paused and then grinned as if she was amused with me.

"When he was sixteen I taught him all about sex. I started his addiction. We fucked on this very table so many times I can't count. I've stood right here with my legs spread while he licked my pussy until I couldn't stand up. I let him be with other girls to get his taste. But I knew he'd always come back here. He wanted me. Needed what I gave him. He's good at sex because I showed him what a woman wants. What she aches for. That mouth you've kissed has been all over this body," she cupped her breast as she said it.

I couldn't find words. The things she was saying sounded like rantings from a crazy woman. She wanted me to believe he'd been having sex with a forty-year-old married woman when he was sixteen?

"You are trying to sink your claws into what is mine."

"You're married," I said still in shock that she'd even think I could believe her.

She laughed at me then. "That doesn't matter. Not to us. Cruz and I crave each other. He was mine until you came along. Now I'm pregnant with his child and he wants nothing to do with me or the baby. You're taking our child's father away." She touched her stomach gently.

"You're lying," I said shaking my head and backing up toward the door. I knew Cruz had been a little wild. That wasn't a secret. But he hadn't done this. I was sure of it.

"I knew you wouldn't believe me," she said and picked up a remote from her desk. The sounds of sex filled the room, and I turned to see the flat screen behind me.

There would be no denying what I watched. Kelsey was naked, her legs wide open and her head thrown back as Cruz screwed her on her desk. Just like she'd said.

"We liked to video our sex and watch it later. It got us hot and bothered. We often fucked while watching us fuck on the screen.

That's the kind of thing Cruz needs to make him truly happy. I also watched him. He would fuck some girl while I hid and watched. He liked knowing I was there while he did it. Seeing them. He'd get so worked up we'd both be crazy for it. I have videos of that too if you need to see."

"Fuck yes, Kelsey. Open wide you dirty whore. Give me what I want," Cruz's words came from the screen and I cringed. "Such a nasty bitch. My nasty little bitch, give me that ass." Cruz then flipped her over. Pulling her hips up so her ass was stuck in the air. He spit on her bottom then stuck his fingers inside. "Tight asshole. You want my dick up that ass, don't you?" She screamed, "Yes, fuck my ass. Fuck it hard!" She turned her head around to look back at him and he covered her mouth with his—that was all I could take. I ran. I ran out the door. I ran to my car. I ran from it all. I drove. I didn't stop. I didn't know where I was going but my soul had been destroyed.

My phone kept ringing but I couldn't answer it. I turned my phone off. If it was my mother I wouldn't be able to speak. She'd be worried. All I could do was drive. Run away from it all. Until my chest didn't feel as if it were crushed.

The words he had said to Kelsey and the image of them together replayed over and over. Nausea clawed at my throat. Disbelief that I had actually trusted him. Thought what we had was real. But he . . . he was darker than I knew. When the tears finally began to fall, I pulled off at an exit and parked in a hotel parking lot. I cried for all I had dreamed of. All the happiness I thought I had found. And all that would forever mark me. I would never be the same. My fantasy had been just that. Nothing had been real. There would be no fond memories. Only one nightmare.

I'm sorry. But I'm okay. I just needed some space. I sent that one text to my mother to keep her from being worried. There were twenty-eight missed texts and fifty missed calls when I turned my phone back on. I ignored them all, turned the phone off again and went to pay for a room for the night.

Chapter Forty-One

~CRUZ KERRINGTON~

I T HAD BEEN sex. That was it. How had I known my affair with Kelsey would lead to this? I kept my head buried in my hands as my father paced in front of me. The room was silent now. His ranting and yelling had ended.

"She's okay. That was Harlow on the phone. Lila Kate sent her a simple text saying she was fine but needed space." My mother announced as she entered the living room.

I looked up for the first time in a while. Relief that Lila Kate was safe helped ease my fears. The pain still tore through my chest. I'd called her and texted her numerous times begging for her to listen to me. She hadn't replied to any of them.

"Did she say where she was?" I asked already knowing the chance of the Carters telling me was slim to none.

Mom shook her head. "No. I think Grant is trying to track her cell phone though."

He was busy worrying about Lila Kate's safety. I knew once she was back here safely he'd come for me. Right now, I hoped he did. I should have dealt with Kelsey. Thinking it would just go away was stupid.

"She is threatening a lawsuit," Dad said. "I've confiscated all the items in her office. The videos were found. There are some when you were underage. Those will protect the club. She will be the one facing charges if she pushes this."

Mom sank to sit on the edge of the chair in front of me. "You were just a baby. She was my age. I just don't understand how she could do that?"

"He was a willing partner, Della," Dad reminded her. "And if she is pregnant then we have that to deal with."

I shook my head. "That baby won't be mine. If there is one."

"But if it is, you aren't a teenage boy anymore being taken advantage of. You're a grown ass man who knew better than to screw around with a married woman."

Mom paled at his words. I'd hurt so many people. How did I think I deserved someone like Lila Kate? After all the shit I'd done.

"I know that," I told him lifting my eyes to meet his. "I should have stopped it. Hell, I shouldn't have started it. But I am paying for it. I love Lila and now I've lost her. She's hurting and it's all my fault. That's killing me."

Dad scowled. "Yes, it is. In life, you're gonna make mistakes but this one is beyond a mistake. It's selfish, irresponsible, and straight up dishonest. That woman is married. I get you were a teenage boy with raging hormones, but she is a married woman. That," he said pointing at me. "That right there was where you messed up. No, Lila Kate won't forgive you. How could she?"

I stood up unable to sit here and listen to my mistakes anymore. I knew I had fucked up. I didn't need my dad reminding me over and over. What I needed to do was find a way to fix this. Which seemed impossible.

"Where are you going?" Dad's anger hadn't dissipated any during the hour he'd been yelling at me.

"Are we not done here?" I shot back.

He closed the space between us and glared at me. "You slept with a married employee of a business that will be yours one day. You made sex videos with her. She's claiming to be pregnant with your child. No, we're not fucking done here. I've spoken with the lawyers. I've spoken with Kelsey's husband. We are meeting in one hour in the club's boardroom. You're not going anywhere."

Lila Kate was out there and I had no idea where or how to find her or where to even look. I'd called Nate but he swore she hadn't come to Sea Breeze. She needed to hear my side of this story. I had to explain it to her. Maybe she'd understand after I had a chance to explain how it all got started and how until I ran after her when she left town I had seen no issue with what I'd done. I did now. If I could just be the man she wanted me to be and erase all the past shit I'd done. I was a fuckup. Now I would pay for it.

"She needs her space. You can't find her anyway. You don't know where she went," my mother's voice was calm and understanding.

"I did this. I hurt her." My voice cracked with emotion as I said it.

My mom nodded. "Yes. And you'll be the only one who can fix it. But for now, you have something else to fix."

"Goddamn right he does," Dad's tone was angry and annoyed.

"Woods, calm down. I know you're angry. But this started when he was a kid. She took advantage of him. Remember that."

Dad threw up his hands in frustration. "She is married, Della. Married. I'd like to think my son has more morals than that."

Mom nodded. "Me too. But what is done is done. We thought his wild streak was just that and he'd outgrow it. We should have been paying closer attention."

Dad pointed at me. "He should have used his damn brain and not his dick!"

Mom winced. "Seriously, honey. Are those words necessary?"

He shook his head. "This is just. Fuck it. I wasn't perfect at his age but I didn't do this. I didn't put the club into legal question. And I didn't screw around with married employees."

But I had.

"When do we leave for the club?" I asked.

"We should leave now. I need to make sure the room is ready. And our lawyers need to go over some things with you. What you can and can't say."

Mom stood up. "I'm going."

"No," Dad and I said at the same time.

Mom frowned. "Why not?"

I looked at Dad, and he sighed. "Because Della, I'm afraid we will be dealing with more legal issues when you see Kelsey. The videos will be discussed and I don't trust you not to attack the woman."

He had a better reason than I did. I'd just been worried it would upset her.

"She's pregnant. It may not be Cruz's child but I'd never hurt a pregnant woman," Mom argued.

Dad raised his eyebrow. "You haven't seen the videos."

Mom let out a deep sigh then nodded. "Perhaps you're right."

Dad walked over to my mom, pulled her into his arms then kissed her head. "I'll keep you posted."

She nodded against his chest. They'd always been like this. Close. One unit. Dad worshiped her, and she adored him. I hadn't wanted that. I always thought it made them vulnerable. I didn't trust that. It was a gamble to love like that. I'd heard how awful most marriages were from Kelsey for years. I believed her.

But watching them I realized I wanted that too. I'd had a taste with Lila Kate. A brief time where I knew she was all I would ever want. Now it was gone too soon. What my parents had wasn't unique to them. It was simply that they loved each other.

Kelsey didn't love. There was the difference.

My parents weren't made vulnerable by their love. They were stronger because of it. My lies and secrets had to come out for me to see and understand that kind of love. Why did that have to be the case? Why couldn't I have realized this years ago and saved so many people the pain?

I wouldn't lose Lila Kate without a fight. I'd heal everything I'd broken the best way I could. I would learn and move on. Then I would find some way for her to forgive me. Even if it took the rest of our lives. I'd wait for her. For us.

Chapter Forty-Two

~ELI HARDY~

WATCHING LILA WALK toward me with the sun-kissed highlights in her hair and perfect features marked with pain, I realized something. She had felt "more." She had experienced that "more" that we all hope for. That intensity that grabs you and holds you so tightly you can't do anything but enjoy the ride and hope for the best.

I wasn't the ride for her. The night I met her she'd already been grabbed by it. Hell, she was already on the ride and didn't want to be. Cruz had snagged her heart a long time ago. But I was thankful her journey had brought her to me. Without her, without my feelings developing for her I would have never believed I could love someone like I loved Bliss. I knew now that I was wrong. Bliss was my best friend, she was my childhood. We were grown now and our ride was over.

Lila stopped at the table I had found us outside the bakery in Sea Breeze. One I'd eaten at many times before. She'd called me two days after Nate came by to see me asking if I had heard from her. I hadn't at the time. But he told me some bad shit went down concerning Cruz and Lila had run.

I had asked her where she was when she had called and she'd told me in Nashville. I thought about going to her. But I didn't. She wasn't mine. She never would be. But this morning I'd gotten a text. She was in Sea Breeze. She wanted to see me.

The dark circles under her lovely eyes and the sadness obvious in her expression pained me. I hated to see her like this. I knew what heartbreak felt like. It was never easy. It destroyed you. Pulling yourself together afterward took strength. And I knew Lila had that strength.

"I ordered your coffee the way you like it," I told her as she sat down across from me.

She attempted a smile. It was weak and didn't meet her eyes. "Thank you."

I watched her take a small sip and then lift her gaze to look at me. "Thanks for meeting me here."

I shrugged. "Had nothing better to do. Sea Breeze has grown boring."

Lila didn't laugh at my attempt to lighten the mood. Instead, I could see her eyes go somewhere else. Her thoughts lost in another moment. I let her go there alone while I drank some of my tea. She was more broken than I'd ever seen a female. Nate had told me the story. What Cruz had done. Why Lila had left and how she'd found out. It was a messy clusterfuck. But after meeting Cruz it didn't surprise me. Nate said he'd known Cruz was fucking that married woman back when they were teens. He hadn't really thought more about it over the years.

"Have you slept any?" I asked bringing her back to the here and now. Not the demons in her head taunting her.

She focused on me again then started to nod and stopped. "No, not really. When I close my eyes . . . I'm there in that room. She's showing me the video . . . I hear them." She stopped and shook her head. "And I know it was before me. I know he was with many, many females before me." She closed her eyes as if she had to say something she didn't want to say. That she couldn't bear to look at me as she said it. "That woman took advantage of him. I don't even blame him completely for the affair. She was the adult for the majority of their . . . relationship." She slowly opened her eyes and met my gaze. "It's the video. The things he said to her," her voice was a whisper. "If that's what he wants. He never said things like that to me. Our sex . . . had to have bored him."

As completely curious as I was to know what he had said during sex that had her so concerned, I asked the obvious question instead. "You're not worried about her being pregnant?"

Lila shook her head. "No. Even if she's pregnant, which I don't believe she is, it's not his. Women have been claiming pregnancy trying to hold on to a man they've lost since the beginning of the human race, I'd guess. At first, I believed her but I was devastated. I've had time to think about her actions. The way she told me. How she said it. She isn't a mentally stable person."

I had to agree with the mentally stable part. If she'd started fucking Cruz when he was sixteen then something was off in her head. "Are you going back soon?" I asked.

She shrugged. "I'll have to eventually. I have my studio to finish. My life to get back to. It's going to be hard. Cruz didn't lie to me because I never asked about his past sexual experiences. But he had known this thing with Kelsey was about to blow up and he didn't tell me. Maybe having sex with her when he was young and stupid can be forgiven. But the video I saw was more recent. He was older. He was still seeing her. How can I trust him if he had no guilt over screwing a married woman?"

She had a point. And I wasn't sure I had an answer for her. What I did know was that everyone had their secrets. Their own darkness. Something they hid from the world. Choosing to forgive them was a choice. Was losing a chance at having that "more" we all wanted worth being unable to forgive? Or could love be enough? To cover all of it and heal them both?

"Do you love Cruz?" I asked her.

She nodded.

"Did this . . . video, or this woman's words kill any of that love? Weaken it in any way?"

She paused then shook her head. Her shoulders drooped sadly as she admitted it.

"Then you owe it to yourself to listen to him and forgive him. If you don't you're only hurting yourself."

Lila's eyes filled with tears. "But I may not be enough to hold him. I'm not . . . I'm not experienced. I don't do things like what I saw and heard. I'm . . . I am boring."

That made me want to laugh. The woman in front of me was anything but boring. But I didn't laugh because I had enough females in my life to know when they say shit like that they believed it. Laughing at it didn't turn out well.

"You are anything but boring. Sure, you're polite, prim, and proper. You're kind and thoughtful. You don't use your beauty as a weapon. You are completely fascinating. Men watch you. They are stunned by you, and you miss it because you're oblivious, which makes you more appealing. Cruz Kerrington and I have very little in common. But the one thing we do is we are both heterosexual males. I know what he sees when he looks at you. I also know that the man came running after you when you had left town. He didn't want to lose you. He loves you, Lila. I saw it at your apartment that morning. Go back. Let him explain."

She gave me a small smile then. "You think all that about me?"

"Every word."

"Why couldn't it have been you? Why did my heart have to love him?"

I laughed then. I wondered the same thing at first but I had time to think about it and I knew I had some things to face. Things to admit to myself. And before this past month, I wouldn't have been ready to move on. I would be wasting my life wanting a woman who was never going to feel the same. I would still be messing up every date I had because I was comparing them to Bliss. But things were different now. I was different.

I had her to thank. It was all because of Lila.

Chapter Forty-Three

♥ LILA KATE ♥

IT HAD TAKEN me three hours to get my parents to leave. Once I texted them that I was home they had come over with food within the hour. They hadn't talked about Cruz or the reason I left. We ate. I told them where all I had gone. It was awkward small talk at first. When my dad mentioned dealing with some issues, I immediately warned him I'd never forgive him if he said or did anything to Cruz. He'd looked very unhappy about that, but with my mother's encouragement, he'd agreed to leave it alone.

Getting them to leave and give me alone time had been another issue. When Ophelia came home they finally left. I let out a sigh of relief when they walked out the door.

"They been here awhile?" she asked as she poured herself a glass of water.

"Yes. But they were worried and needed to know I was okay. Just glad that's over."

Ophelia walked over and sat down across from me on the sofa. "You talk to him?"

I knew the him she was referring to was Cruz. I shook my head.

"You going to?" she asked.

I had thought about everything Eli had said on my way home yesterday. "Yes. Eventually. We will have to talk."

"Kelsey wasn't pregnant," she said watching me closely to see my reaction.

"I never really thought she was. But how do they know?"

"Mom said that Woods threatened to press charges for child pornography. She had videos in her office of sex with . . . well, when he was sixteen."

I couldn't respond to that. I hated those videos.

"Sorry . . . I shouldn't have brought it up but I thought you would want to know. I mean, I was shocked you were with Cruz. The two of you, well, you don't really fit. He's Cruz. Sex videos, a different woman every night, drunk partying Cruz."

That was all people saw when they looked at Cruz. What he'd done. Not who he was. Had anyone ever looked closely enough to care? Anyone but me?

"He's smart, and he's thoughtful. He has a big heart and he doesn't mean to hurt anyone. He loves his family. He doesn't want to disappoint his dad. There is a lot more to Cruz than what he's done."

Ophelia sat quietly, her eyes studying me. "You really do love him, don't you?" It wasn't a question.

"My loving him isn't the question. What worries me is if that is enough."

Ophelia got up and walked over to me and put her arm around me. "It's about finding your own twisted perfection, letting yourself fall too far and taking a chance. If you've done all that. You have no reason to give up. Not now."

"What if it's not giving up but accepting reality?" I asked her.

She smiled. "You don't know what that reality is just yet."

That all sounded easy. But I knew none of it was. Loving Cruz was like playing with a very hot flame. I was going to get burned eventually. I went to sleep that night wondering if that was worth it.

One week later, I realized all my worry over forgiving him was pointless. Cruz hadn't come to talk to me. He hadn't called to check on me. All the voicemails and texts begging me to forgive him the day I left were it. He never called or texted again. This town wasn't small. He knew I was back and he wasn't coming to explain. He wasn't doing anything.

I spent the days working in the studio, ordered take out, cried in the shower until I was too tired to cry anymore and then went to bed. It had become a routine. My mom had called about us having lunch but I'd told her I was too busy. She was eventually going to show up with food at the studio one day.

Ophelia left for Sea Breeze with her family. They were going to visit Nate and Bliss for a few weeks. The apartment was quiet. All I had were my thoughts, and those were always about Cruz. I was starting to look forward to the day I could take a shower and not cry until there were no tears left. I wanted my happiness back.

The painting was done. Mirrors were being installed along with bars along the walls. Next would be the floor. The sounds of construction and workers gave me something to focus on other than Cruz.

When week two since my return came to a close, I didn't cry in the shower. I watched a movie before bed and ate an entire meal instead of just nibbling. Staring at the ceiling that night I realized my life was going to be okay. Cruz wasn't coming to see me. But I needed the closure. His actions or non-action told me what I needed to know about us. He was finished. I had a few things to say to him first.

I would get up in the morning, and I'd find Cruz. I would give us the closure I needed. Then I would finally put Cruz Kerrington behind me. I'd move on, and this time I wouldn't look back.

Chapter Forty-Four
~CRUZ KERRINGTON~

HAPPIER. LILA KATE was happier. I had watched her. I went to Sea Breeze even after Nate had told me she wasn't there—I'd found her. She'd been there. She'd been happier. Eli had sat across from her and she was smiling. He'd laughed. They'd been free of guilt, darkness, and pain. Lila Kate belonged with him. Accepting it had been painful. I wanted her to be happy. I had hurt her in a way he never would. I needed her. But she needed him. I loved her more than any man ever would.

That didn't matter. Seeing her smile. Laugh. It had all been so clear. She needed him. Not me. Fucked up Cruz Kerrington didn't deserve Lila Kate. She'd have someone new. Someone who wouldn't break her heart. I wanted her to be happy. Leaving her there with him had been one of the hardest things I'd done. But she'd come home. And now here I was.

I'd watched her for two weeks. She didn't leave. Worked all day, ordered out food, then went to bed early. More than a dozen times I'd almost got out of this damn work truck I was using from the club's course maintenance department and walked over there and knocked on the door. But I couldn't. She hadn't called. She hadn't come to find me. Not even a text.

My past was more than she could accept. But what could I have expected? Lila Kate wasn't tarnished in any way. She'd never messed up. I was her only fucking regret. I took a drink of the coffee I had resorted to drinking because I couldn't sleep at night and the exhaustion that came with it required caffeine.

My dad didn't want me at the club. He'd said I had a lot of growing up to do and now that the issue with Kelsey was handled and she was gone, he decided it was best that I had no dealings with the club other than working on the lawn care crew for the golf course.

I was up at four in the morning cutting grass, weed eating, and cleaning up trash seven days a week. Dad said if I didn't want to do that and work my way up the ladder the hard way, I was welcome to find another future. The club meant too much for him to entrust it to me after exposing my immoral behavior.

I'd forgotten the piece of cake in my hand that I'd gotten from the coffee shop when I saw Lila Kate walk outside for the first time in two weeks. I dropped it on the floorboard and sat my cup down as she made her way to her car. She was going somewhere. Was she going back to him? Leaving this place for Sea Breeze? Panic settled in even when I knew she deserved what Eli Hardy could give her.

Once she pulled out, I followed her. I realized this wasn't healthy, but I had decided I was fucked in the head like my dad said. I needed therapy or something. I figured this lawn care shit before the sun came up was good therapy.

It didn't take me long to figure out she was headed to my house, not Sea Breeze. Right before she turned into my driveway she pulled off the road and I slowed the truck down. Her car door swung open and she turned to look at me with her hands on her hips as if she was annoyed.

I pulled over behind her, turned the truck off and climbed out.

"Are you following me around?" she asked. "Do you think sunglasses and a baseball cap is an actual disguise?"

I thought it had hidden me enough. I was driving this dusty old truck too. I was impressed she had paid that close of attention to her surroundings to realize she was being followed. "Yeah."

"Why?" she demanded.

"I was worried about you." And trying to build the nerve to talk to you. But I didn't say that.

Lila Kate stalked toward me and both her small hands shoved me hard in the chest. "I've been back two weeks. That's all you have to say?" she yelled shoving me back again. "You were worried about me? Why CRUZ? Why were you worried about me? Because your insane married friend showed me fuck videos of the two of you and told me she was pregnant with your kid?" Lila Kate was getting louder, and her eyes were filling with tears. I reached out to touch her arms. To hold her back from pushing me into the road and to try and calm her.

"NO! Don't touch me. You don't get to touch me! I loved you! And you wait for two weeks, sitting outside my place and watch me!"

She knew I'd sat outside her place? Damn. She was more perceptive than I gave her credit for.

Tears were flowing freely down her face now. She sobbed and hit me with her fists. Once on the arm and another on the chest. After she pummeled me, she spun around and started to run back to her car.

"You said loved," I called out. "That's past tense, Lila Kate. Is it over? Do you love someone else that soon?" Fear was clogging my throat. I'd watched her while holding on to the small shred of hope that she'd forgive me. That she hadn't moved on so quickly to Eli Hardy. That she still loved me. Not being able to love me after what she saw, what she knew, was worse. How did I fight for her if she didn't love me?

She stopped. We both stood there. Her back to me. I waited even though I want to run to her. To hold her. To beg her to love me.

"What do you want from me?" she asked turning back to me. Her tear-streaked face was blotchy and red.

"Everything," I replied honestly.

"Where have you been?"

"Outside your place. In that damn truck," I admitted.

"Why?"

"Because I was terrified of this. That I had no chance to make it right. That I'd lost it all. That I'd lost you."

"So you didn't come ask me? You let me think it was done?"

I shook my head. "I called and texted you and you never replied. I was waiting. Giving you time. And . . . I saw you with him. I saw you smile. I saw you laugh. You were happy, Lila. I want you to be happy. I didn't leave you though. I was right outside the whole time. Except when I am cutting grass and weed eating at four in the morning on the golf course."

"You saw me smiling with who?" she asked confusion on her face.

"Eli."

"Eli? In Sea Breeze?"

"I came looking for you. I found you. With him. He made you smile. He's good. He hasn't hurt you like I did."

She didn't reply at first. She just stood there staring at me letting my confession sink in. She couldn't deny what I had seen. How Eli had made her forget the pain. He'd given her a reason to smile. He would never hurt her like I had but. We both knew he could never love her like I did. No one could.

"When was the last time you were with her?" she asked me.

"Three months ago. I was hammered. She called me. I went to her. It was a habit. One I will regret for the rest of my life."

"At first, did you love her?"

"I was a kid, Lila. I loved any female who would let me stick my dick in her vagina. Then she started telling me how mistreated she was and how her husband wouldn't have sex with her. I felt sorry for her. At one point, I think I thought we were friends but it was always manipulation on her part. I never loved her. I've been in love once. I still am. Even when I didn't realize it, Lila, it was you. Always you. The girl I never felt good enough for. The girl I watched from afar and dreamed about at night. Just you."

She sniffled and wiped away a single tear. "I'm afraid you'll get bored with me. We're so different. I . . . I'm not as experienced or adventurous. I could be, but I don't even know how."

My chest felt lighter than it had in weeks. I took my first deep breath since the moment I found out Lila Kate was missing and why. "Are you serious?" I asked taking a step toward her.

She nodded.

"Do you have any idea how perfect you are for me?"

She shook her head this time.

"There has not been one time in my life I didn't think about my future and see you in it. Your face was always there. Your voice in my head when I was doing the wrong thing. Those eyes would haunt me even when I was passed out drunk. You have been with me every moment of my life. Even if I didn't want you there, my heart held onto you. My soul found its mate when I was a kid. I might have fought against it but the connection was made. It always will be." I took another step toward her. "You can hate me. You can never forgive me. You can tell me to leave and not come back. But I'll love you forever. That won't change."

She sniffled again. "Does that mean you'll sit outside like

some stalker watching me?"

I grinned. "Most likely, yes."

Lila Kate closed the small distance between us and put her hands on my chest gently this time. "That doesn't leave me any choice then does it."

"Are you going to get a restraining order?" I teased.

She smiled then. The big beautiful smile that had been making my knees weak for as long as I could remember. "That's an option," she replied. "But I think I'll go with option number two."

"And that is?" I asked.

She stood on her tiptoes and pressed a kiss to my jawline. "To love you the rest of my life."

I held her face in my hands and stared down at the woman who would always be what made me whole. She was my center. Loving her had destroyed me. The old me was gone. The careless, selfish man I'd been was no longer there. I wanted to be good enough for her. And I would be. I would be the kind of man my father was. My life had purpose.

All because of Lila.

ABBI GLINES

ABBI GLINES IS a #1 New York Times, USA Today, and Wall Street Journal bestselling author of the Rosemary Beach, Sea Breeze, Vincent Boys, Existence, and The Field Party Series . She never cooks unless baking during the Christmas holiday counts. She believes in ghosts and has a habit of asking people if their house is haunted before she goes in it. She drinks afternoon tea because she wants to be British but alas she was born in Alabama. When asked how many books she has written she has to stop and count on her fingers. When she's not locked away writing, she is reading, shopping (major shoe and purse addiction), sneaking off to the movies alone, and listening to the drama in her teenagers lives while making mental notes on the good stuff to use later. Don't judge.

You can connect with Abbi online in several different ways. She uses social media to procrastinate.

www.abbiglines.com
www.facebook.com/abbiglinesauthor
twitter.com/AbbiGlines
www.instagram.com/abbiglines
www.pinterest.com/abbiglines

Other titles by
ABBI GLINES

ROSEMARY BEACH SERIES

Fallen Too Far

Never Too Far

Forever Too Far

Rush Too Far

Twisted Perfection

Simple Perfection

Take A Chance

One More Chance

You Wc're Mine

Kiro's Emily

When I'm Gone

When You're Back

The Best Goodbye

Up In Flames

SEA BREEZE SERIES

Breathe

Because of Low

While It Lasts

Just For Now

Sometimes It Lasts

Misbehaving

Bad For You

Hold On Tight

Until The End

SEA BREEZE MEETS ROSEMARY BEACH
Like A Memory
Because of Lila

THE FIELD PARTY SERIES
Until Friday Night
Under the Lights
After the Game (Coming August 22, 2017)

ONCE SHE DREAMED
Once She Dreamed (Part 1)
Once She Dreamed (Part 2)

THE VINCENT BOYS SERIES
The Vincent Boys
The Vincent Brothers

THE MASON DIXON SERIES
Boys South of the Mason Dixon

EXISTENCE TRILOGY
Existence (Book 1)
Predestined (Book 2)
Leif (Book 2.5)
Ceaseless (Book 3)

Printed in Great Britain
by Amazon

48191550R00142